The Queens of Space

The Queens of Heaven
Book 3

Andrew S. French

Neonoir Books

Also by Andrew S. French

Science Fiction

The Time Traveller's Murder

The Mercy Sleep

Bodies

The Arcane Supernatural Thriller Series

Book one: The Arcane

Book two: The Arcane Identity

Book three: The Arcane Quest

Book four: The Arcane Ultimatum

The Ella Finn Fantasy Novella Series

Ella and the Elementals

Ella and the Multiverse

Ella and the Monsters

Ella and the Dreamers

Supernatural Short Stories

Dead Souls

Dead Souls II

The Shadow

Writing as A. S. French

Crime Fiction and Thrillers

The Astrid Snow series

Book one: Don't Fear the Reaper

Book two: The Killing Moon

Book three: Lost in America

Book four: Gone to Texas

Book five: The Final Girl

The Ophelia Red series

Book one: Ophelia Red

The Detective Jen Flowers series

Book one: The Hashtag Killer

Book two: Serial Killer

Book three: Night Killer

Book four: The Killer Inside Them

The Frank Walker series

Where The Bodies Are Buried

Bodies of Evidence

Crime Short Stories

Crime Stories: A Collection

Call Me: An Astrid Snow Short Story

Dark Snow: An Astrid Snow Short Story

Bette Davis Eyes: Detective Flowers Short Story

Go to www.andrewsfrench.com for more information.

Chapter 1

Kaladan

It's hard to get lost when you don't know where you're from.

Yet all that mattered was where I stood.

Kaladan.

The Gleaming Planet, the Glittering Prize.

It owed its existence to the wealth showered upon it for its unmatched medical knowledge and expertise. Its patrons liked to think of it as the place that postponed death. Its practitioners extended lifespans way beyond their natural limit, but not forever. And there I was, a near-immortal, about to commit my second crime on the planet.

Its capital lay in front of me, a shimmering buzz of a thousand lights and magnificent buildings. The city's noise created a hum that tickled the device attached to my spine. The capital's vast illuminations mostly obscured the dark of the night, but below me were dozens of glowing green lanterns circling the centre of the great city. I removed my spy glasses to get a closer look at them, gasping when I saw decapitated heads in the middle of each one.

Revolutionaries.

Tyranny had ruled Kaladan for thousands of years and would continue long into the future when I became a fugitive on this planet. Despite that, some always rose to fight back – but their resistance could never last because the forces wielded by the ruling elite outnumbered them. So bringing democracy to Kaladan had been on my to-do list for a while. But, unfortunately, I'd got nowhere with it since I couldn't figure out how to bring about those changes without causing more harm.

It would be another five hundred years before an expedition from Earth would reach Kaladan, and it would be the worst mistake my species would ever make. The Kaladanians sold their skills to the highest bidder, their planet constructed around a hierarchical caste system run as a totalitarian dictatorship. They wouldn't need the peace the human emissaries would bring with them, using the information and technology their visitors brought to travel back to Earth and conquer it. It was a long-term problem that needed fixing. That fix was on my schedule, but I had to deal with my present difficulties first.

I stopped looking at the decapitated heads and fought against the itch irritating my neck, wondering if Ishtar knew where I was because of the device in my brain. Maybe she was sitting in my mind's shadows monitoring everything I did. That whole thing with Ursula in the Blitz could have been a ruse to get me to this planet, a trail of breadcrumbs designed to spy on me: to manipulate me. Perhaps even to kill me, so my head ended up like those in the lanterns.

I punched my palm and stared across the glistening city, standing in the hills above Kaladan's capital, Leatham. A rainbow of lights shimmered over the landscape. The man I needed to get this thing out of my head was down there. He was the planet's greatest surgeon, one of its most influential people, and as close to the top of the food chain as a Kaladanian could get without being royalty.

He was also in prison.

My timing was out, arriving during his trial. So, suitably disguised at his show trial, I listened to the evidence against him. He was unmoving and unresponsive during the whole thing, his lips only moving once as they led him from the court. Kaladan's government broadcasted everything across their empire, including showing their cowed citizens the prisoner's cell. It was all the information I needed as I found the trigger and hopped into his future.

'Dr Zante,' I said as I appeared inside his cell. He was surprisingly unalarmed.

'How did you get in here? This is a maximum security facility with unbreakable protections.'

I didn't have time to explain the finer details of what I could do.

I stepped forward and showed him my hands. 'I've come to rescue you.'

'You're not Kaladanian,' he said in surprise.

Kaladanians were much like humans in shape and biology, apart from two things: one of which was that they had one more finger on each hand than us. It was another reason they were the finest surgeons in the universe.

'I need you to remove something from my skull.'

I handed him the communicator with scans of my head and medical details.

He gave it a cursory glance before handing it back. 'You must leave.'

'It should be an easy job for you, Dr Zante.'

His laugh was throaty and sounded like water roaring at the bottom of a cascade.

'And where would I do it?'

He spread his arms around the grim surroundings of cold concrete and dusty shadows.

'Your lab is under quarantine, so nobody will bother us there.' I'd already checked it for suitability. He shook the laughter from his face, his skin so tight it looked like he hadn't smiled in some time.

'I have to pay for my crimes. There's no escaping from this, regardless of where you're from and what technology you have.'

'Crimes? You risked your life to save those infected people working in the sewers. I wouldn't call what you did crimes.'

He stared at me as if I was a child. I guess, to his eyes, I was.

'Then you know little of this world and how it works, stranger. I cured those poor folk by using medicine not intended for them. They couldn't afford what I stole. Nothing is free on Kaladan. You work, and you earn, or you suffer and die.'

The finality of his words was a grim shadow in a room full of ominous portent.

'So why did you do it?'

4

He shifted his body on the bed, his face moving towards me, the bruises under his eyes sparkling in greater detail.

'In life, one has to stand up for what is right. My sacrifice will have been for nothing if you take me from here.'

Enlightenment hit me. 'That's why you never spoke at your trial – you wanted to highlight the system's injustice.'

He laughed again. 'The system? There is no system on Kaladan, young woman. The people are ruled by a tyrant, his family, and other families who have committed their crimes for a thousand years. But it will all change soon, and I can't risk that by escaping from this cell.'

There was pride in his voice, and it shocked me. I'd missed the essential details in this brave man's life. 'You're part of a resistance?'

I'd never heard of such a thing on Kaladan. Not now, and not two hundred years in the future, when I would become a criminal for the first time on the planet, and not half a millennium from now, when humanity would set foot on Kaladan and regret it.

How could I tell him his sacrifice would be for nothing?

'Are you a spy?' His tone turned harsh. 'Is that how you got through the security to get me to betray the others?'

He moved back against the wall. I had no choice but to use what I knew, and he didn't.

'Don't you want to see your wife again?'

Even in the gloom, I saw his face crumple under the weight of what he was about to lose.

'I've disgraced her. She's better off without me.'

What I was about to tell him weighed heavy on my heart, but there was no other option. I couldn't rescue Diana without getting this device out of my head, and I couldn't do that without him.

'And what about your child, Dr Zante?'

'What?' He moved back into the light, eyes blazing with desperation and confusion.

The other difference between humans and Kaladanians: their females can only give birth once.

'The authorities will come here and tell you tonight, a few hours before your execution, just enough time for you to suffer about what could have been.'

'How do you know this?' The scorn in his voice told me he didn't believe me.

'I know your wife will give birth to twin boys.' The shock knocked him backwards. The birth of twins on Kaladan was one in ten thousand. 'I know a descendent of yours will save my life in two hundred years, and I owe them a debt I can never repay.'

Her name would be Zara, just like his wife. She would be one of the most extraordinary biological anomalies across the known universe: a telekinetic, able to move anything with her mind. His hands trembled, and his head slumped into his lap. He sobbed long and loud before looking at me.

'This cannot be.'

'I can reunite you with your wife, get you far away from this city and help you start a new life in obscurity. You'll be at the lowest level of the social pyramid, but you'll be together and have a future.'

'Zara will give birth to twins?'

'You and your wife will have two boys. They'll do great things with their lives, whether or not you're with them. The choice is yours, Dr Zante.'

My words were harsher than I intended, but they had the desired effect.

'You can travel through time and space?'

'Yes.'

'Then prove it to me now. Disappear and then reappear on the other side of the cell.'

I shook my head. 'If I did that, the release of energy so close to the jumps would cripple me.'

He stared at me as if I was talking about pulling a rabbit out of a hat. Not that I was sure they even had anything like rabbits on this planet.

'How is this energy released that allows you to journey across space and time?'

I sighed. 'Dr Zante, there's no time for this. Will you come with me or not?' I wouldn't force him. I wasn't God, no matter what some others thought.

'You said you've met a descendent of mine, Zara?'

'Yes. She's the spitting image of your wife. But don't ask me about her or the future because I can't tell you.' So there was me sticking to a rule, and it felt weird.

'What's your name?' he said.

'Ruby. Ruby Quartz.'

'How much do you know about my life, Ruby?'

I reached into my perfect memory and the books and clips I'd studied about this man when I met Zara two hundred years in the future.

'I know everything, Dr Zante.' All apart from him being part of the resistance. Perhaps Zara didn't know either.

'Do you know what I said to my wife when I proposed to her?'

Of course I didn't. 'No.'

He smiled at me. 'Tell me that, and I'll consider leaving here with you.'

'Okay.' I searched through the information I had on him and found the time and location of that proposal. 'I'll be back in five minutes.'

I vanished and reappeared behind a tree in the garden

where he proposed to Zara. It was ten years in the past from where I'd just been. The Kaladanian sun warmed my face as I inched closer to the loving couple, listening as he spoke to her. Then a thought struck me: could I get this younger version of Dr Zante to remove the device in my brain?

And leave the future one in prison?

No, I couldn't. I had one plan, and I was going to stick to it – there would be no more recklessness from me.

I returned five minutes after leaving him in prison, the hairs on my arms and neck bristling as I landed in the cell.

Zante gazed at me. 'I saw no energy release when you disappeared, Ruby Quartz.'

'Believe me, Doc, it's here. I can feel it in my bones.' And the flattened Time Ring vibrated on my spine.

'What did I say to my wife?' he said.

'You told Zara your greatest wish had been to change the world, to rid Kaladan of all its tyrants. That was until you met her, and she changed yours.'

His lips shook as he spoke. 'You can make us all disappear?'

I nodded. 'I promise.'

'Then do it. I have to be with my children, whatever the consequences.'

I studied him, the expectant father. He'd sacrificed himself to help the poorest people on this planet, including abandoning his wife. But now everything had changed for him.

Would parents do anything for their offspring?

I took his hand, and we vanished. We reappeared downstairs in his house. I let him go to the wife I'd brought to the house earlier, as I ensured that outside the building was free of government agents. The front looked out onto other houses, and everywhere was empty. It was the same around the back, looking out to a vast swampland. The building had as much illumination as the city we'd just left, brilliant lights in contrast to the endless darkness leading away from it.

I returned to the house, about to trust one of the foremost surgeons in the universe. But one who had never operated on a human brain. I sucked in the air and stared at the symbols on my wrists. In my mind, there were only visions of what I'd seen before, of the experiments the Queens of Heaven had forced Diana to perform upon Ursula. And of me lying face down as Dash sliced my back open.

Did everything connect to me on an operating table?

Zante came downstairs. 'Follow me into the basement.'

I did, with one question burning in my mind. 'How does it feel to know you'll be a father?'

He stared at me, straining to control his emotions. Maybe he needed to be focused on what he was about to do to my brain, or perhaps he was overcome by what his wife had just confirmed. But he didn't answer.

Watching his face twist and turn, knowing he was thinking now as a prospective parent, made me focus on my alleged heritage. Was I a grandmother who had wiped the mind of a younger version of me so I could be eternally young? Is that why I'd lost so many memories? Because remembering a previous life would only be a burden if you regained your youth. Was that why I couldn't remember my mother and father?

'You must take these.' He handed me two small pills. I looked at them with suspicion. 'They will put you out during the operation.'

It was too late not to trust him. I slipped them down my dry throat, a bitter taste hitting the pit of my stomach. I climbed on the table, the sparkle on the laser scalpel the last thing I saw.

* * *

There was a low throb at the back of my skull when I woke.

'You must know people in high places on this planet, which is impressive for an alien.'

He sat opposite me when I rose from my enforced slumber. I rubbed at my head, expecting more pain but pleasantly surprised there was none.

'Why do you say that?'

I stared in the mirror, searching for a scar, but I looked as good as new. Then I found it near my ear. He threw the communication device on the table, some of my blood still clinging to it. The smell of copper lingered in the air.

'The technocrats of the royal court manufactured this. Only the Empress, her family, and a few select courtiers have access to this tech: unless you stole it.'

His words sent shivers down my spine. What had Dash promised them? What guarantees had she given the most brutal rulers in the universe?

I ran my fingers over my scalp, finding the spot where my hair used to be and the new scar. I smiled and wondered where the knife would kiss me next.

'You did a good job, Doc.'

He peered at me with a curious expression. 'Which planet are you from?'

I threw water into my eyes, glad to have my thoughts only to myself again.

'It doesn't matter, Dr Zante. Thank you for what you've done. Now I need to get you and your wife to a new location.'

I had the perfect spot for them on the other side of Kaladan. I knew it well two centuries into the future. But he slipped out of my grip and stopped me.

'How is it possible for you to travel through time and space? Even the cleverest scientists on Kaladan have failed to construct a working teleporter.'

His fingers trembled as his scientific brain struggled to understand how I'd transported him and his wife to their house.

'It's only an accident of biology, Doc.'

Should I tell him about his telekinetic descendant, a woman who would be one in ten thousand? I decided not to burden him with more mysteries.

'Do all your species have brains like yours?'

'What do you mean?'

'There's energy in your brain I've never seen in any other creature.'

A nagging doubt niggled away at the back of my skull as he spoke.

'What type of energy?'

Excitement gripped his eyes, driven, I expected, by the new scientific inscrutability thrust upon him by my arrival. However, his imprisonment and life as a fugitive appeared to be the last things on his mind.

'The neurons in your brain vibrate on a peculiar frequency. I assumed it was something to do with your species. I didn't want to spend too much time inside your skull, but I saw another odd thing.'

He left his words hanging.

Before I could ask the question, his wife ran across the room and threw her arms around me. She sobbed into my chest and couldn't stop thanking me until Dr Zante pulled her away.

'We'll go to your new home soon,' I said as I took him to one side. 'What was this unusual thing on my brain, Doc?'

He scratched at his beard and stared into my eyes.

'It was at the bottom of your cerebellum. It looked like part of it was burnt.'

Before I could say anything, the wall behind me split apart in a terrifying explosion.

Chapter 2

The Sound of Time

The force of the explosion hurled me across the room. I hit the wall and cracked my shoulder. Dust was everywhere, and the howling of a thousand bells filled my ears. I scrambled up and looked for Dr Zante and his wife, unable to see anything through the fog of debris.

Then somebody grabbed my arm and threw me to the floor. I rolled over broken glass, with shards sticking into my hands and arms. Instinct sent my mind searching for the trigger to get me out of there.

But I couldn't leave the Zantes. I'd promised them a new life.

As I considered getting out and returning three minutes into the future, thick fingers grabbed my throat and choked me. My face and neck were on fire, electricity flashing through every inch of me. Then, my thoughts turned to fog, and it was impossible to reach that trigger. My attacker's nails cut into my skin, drawing blood that ran onto him. I lifted a hand to claw him off me, but I didn't have the strength.

'Don't kill her,' somebody shouted.

He mumbled something, stopped, and lessened his grip. My vision blurred, with human shapes drifting in and out of sight. The place stank of smoke and burning rubber as I brought my foot down and stamped on him, sending him falling away from me. I heard several feet stomping into the room and knew it was time to go. I'd return with Dash and enough future weapons to wipe whoever this was off the face of the planet.

As that thought sparked my brain into action, something hard struck my throat, right where the bloke had been choking me. I struggled to breathe and clawed at the object, my fingers slipping from the metal attached to my neck. My back was against the wall as I continued clawing at it, then stumbled forward as the cloud of dust and smoke dissipated. Somebody hit me again, punching my cheek, so I crashed to the floor. I searched for the trigger in my head, but nothing was there.

'Secure the room,' a man's voice said. The same person had given the order not to kill me. I crawled across the broken glass and debris, looking for Dr Zante and his wife but unable to find them. Were they restrained as I was?

Then he spoke again. 'Are you going to stay on the floor like the dog you are?'

Pain shot through me as I peered into the face of a man famous on Kaladan and several planets in this solar system: Riz Orme, the Butcher of Cassan. I'd never met him before, but I knew his history from my excursion to this planet two hundred years into its future. Then, he was a legendary hero for Kaladan's authoritarian rulers. Now, he was a young man, only in his mid-thirties, but a lifetime of experience had aged his face, creating thin cheekbones, sallow skin, and small eyes sunk into pits of darkness. There was no joy in him, but he smiled at me. He looked away as a uniformed soldier carrying a gun approached him.

'We haven't apprehended the fugitives yet, Commander.'

Orme's voice bristled with anger. 'Don't disappoint me, soldier.' Then he returned his gaze to me. 'Are you wondering what it is around your neck, child?' He didn't wait for a reply that I struggled to give, instead removing a small device from his pocket. 'You should feel the fleeting vibrations running through your skin and bones. Those are energy suppressors stopping you from teleporting out of here.'

It stopped pressing against my throat, and I found my voice. 'How did you know we were here?'

More soldiers stepped through the wall, and he instructed them to search the place. I hoped Dr Zante and his wife had escaped.

Orme pointed above my head. 'We have cameras in every building on the planet, including inside his prison cell. And I stationed my men here after we learnt of Zante's traitorous actions with the Resistance.'

A soldier pushed Zante into the room, followed by his

wife. There was no fear on their faces, only a resigned look of inevitability. I'd failed them both: them and their unborn children. I dug my fingers into the debris underneath me and wondered how I'd escape this mess. My spine tingled, and I reached for the trigger in my mind, the switch that could take me anywhere in space and time.

But it wasn't there.

I kept trying, straining my brain until my skull throbbed.

And still, nothing happened.

It was the same result as when Elric Oban fired a suppressing mechanism at my chest on Earth's Moon not so long ago. My fingers touched the metal around my throat. It was tight against my skin, but I could breathe. Was it the same technology that Oban had used on me? If it were, I wouldn't be able to remove it without the controlling device.

But I could do it.

And I let the Butcher of Cassan know. 'You'll be sorry when I get this off.'

Orme glared at me. 'That will never happen, girl.' He slipped the control into his jacket and moved closer to me so I could see the tiny scar below his right eye. His musky smell was mixed with the stink of the explosion that had taken down the wall.

'Stranger things have happened,' I said.

He must have seen me staring at that wound. 'Do you know how I got this?'

As I thought of an answer, two of his men dragged me up and held me like puppeteers playing with a marionette.

'You kissed a rat, and he didn't like it?'

I waited for him to send a shock through my neck bracelet, but nothing came.

'When I was twelve, I argued with my twin brother

about which of us loved our father the most.' He touched the scar on his face. 'My father had the same mark as this, so what better way to show my love than to carve it here? My brother baulked at the thought, but I didn't.' He removed a large knife from his belt, moving it close to my eye. 'Cutting into my flesh made my brother sick, but I enjoyed it.'

I smiled at him. 'It's a good job your dad's scar didn't look like somebody's genitals. Then again....'

The men threw me to the ground, kicking me in the stomach and spine. Rivets of pain invaded every part of me until Orme ordered them to stop. I rolled onto my back and caught my breath before the soldiers dragged me up again.

The knife was still in his grip. 'Where are you from, child?'

I spat blood on the floor. 'Well, you see, there's this lovely village south of here where everyone is kind to each other. You've probably never heard of it, but....'

He lifted his hand for me to stop talking. 'You're not from Kaladan or any of the planets in our Empire. So, where are you from, and how did you get past the orbiting security satellites?'

I shrugged as the men gripped my arms. 'Perhaps I'm just a figment of your imagination.'

'You must have a ship somewhere in orbit, but you also possess a teleportation apparatus. How is that possible, alien child?'

I licked the blood from my lips. 'If you let my friends and me go, I might tell you.'

He nodded to the soldiers, and they checked my clothes, searching for the non-existent teleport device. It only made them dig their fingers harder into my arms. I searched again for the trigger in my brain, finding the same fruitless results.

'Dr Zante and his pitiful wife are not your friends, girl.

They are traitors to the Empire, and their unborn offspring will suffer for it. You'll receive the same fate – executed on a live broadcast shown across the seven planets – once I've got the information I need from you.' He moved closer and touched my face. 'It will take a long time, and you'll eventually endure unmanageable torture and reveal everything. Then the armies of the great Kaladan Empire will find your planet and lay waste to it. Your family and friends will suffer and die because of you.'

'If you're trying to charm the information out of me, you're failing badly.'

More soldiers dragged Zante and his wife near me. He avoided my gaze, but she peered straight at me, begging for help with her eyes. I'd recovered from the shock of the attack, but there were too many of them.

'Remove them all and search the rest of the house,' Orme instructed his men.

I dug my feet into the ground as they tried to haul me out. 'Wait!'

The Butcher of Cassan stared at me. 'Are you ready to cooperate?'

I swallowed the last of the blood in my mouth. 'Let them go, and I'll tell you everything about the secret of teleportation.'

It was a bluff, but it was all I had left.

And it didn't work.

'Torture the traitors first,' Orme instructed his men. 'Leave the alien child to me.'

I was ready to shout again when the sound of a thousand banshees erupted in the room.

Everybody dropped to the floor, including me. The pain started in my ears, quickly transferring to the rest of my head, spreading through every inch of me. It blurred my vision but not enough to realise I'd made a mistake: not everyone was on their knees suffering.

Dr Zante and his wife helped me up. He gave me two small spheres.

'Put these in your ears, and it will block the frequency.'

I did as he suggested, getting instant protection from that terrible howl. My skull continued to ache, but I was okay. And a lot better than those writhing on the floor, including the Butcher of Cassan.

'Is this your doing?' I said to Zante.

He dragged his wife and me away from the intruders towards the hole in the wall.

'It's a weapon the Resistance only developed in the last three months, but Zara and I inserted the plugs into our heads after you brought us here.'

'You knew an attack was coming?'

'It was always a possibility.' He inched nearer the gap and looked outside. 'All of his troops are incapacitated. So we have to leave.'

I pulled at the restraint around my neck. 'Can you get this off me?'

He shook his head. 'Unfortunately, no.'

The metal vibrated against my fingers. Then I glanced behind me, watching Riz Orme squirming on the floor. The blood from his ears had turned his cheeks and chin red. I bent over him, removing the control device from his pocket. I pressed it as I pointed it at the object around my neck.

Nothing happened.

'The sonic disruptor negates all electrical equipment within five hundred yards of the transmission.'

Of course it did. 'Will this work when we get away from the signal?'

'It should.' He didn't sound convincing.

I slipped the device into my jacket before bending to remove the blade from Orme's trembling fingers. At least I'd have one weapon that worked. I smiled at Orme.

'I guess this isn't what you expected tonight.' I pointed the knife at his eye. 'It's not the same as butchering those women and children on Cassan, is it?'

Blood and mucus dribbled from his nose as his eyes burnt into mine.

Dr Zante grabbed my arm. 'We have to leave.'

I wriggled from his grasp. 'So, where do we go from here?'

Zante led us through the gap in the wall. Dozens of soldiers lay writhing on the ground, grasping at their heads as blood leaked from their ears.

'Follow me,' he said as he took us around to the back of the building.

I gazed across the landscape, a vast expanse of dark land that stretched into the horizon.

'Are the Resistance out there?'

Zara Zante spoke. 'No. They're broadcasting that signal from half a mile away on the other side of the house, but they can't keep it going for long without risking capture. So we'll have to make our way across the swampland on our own.'

As soon as she mentioned the swamp, its smell invaded my nose, an aroma of wet earth and thick mud.

'What's stopping Orme and his soldiers from following us?' I said.

'The dark,' Dr Zante said. 'They won't enter the dark.'

Before I could ask why, his wife grabbed his hand and dragged him toward that darkness.

I had no choice but to follow.

Chapter 3

The Ordeal of Kronos

We paused on the dark edge, my feet only inches from the swamp.

'Be careful where you walk,' Dr Zante said.

I peered into the gloom. 'Is there quicksand in there?'

The sonic attack stopped as I asked that question.

Zara Zante pointed at my head. 'You can remove your earplugs.'

I did, dropping them into my pocket if I needed them again. The cold handle of Orme's knife chilled my fingers as

I heard the soldiers behind us. As I turned to them, the Butcher of Cassan grinned at me through bloodied teeth.

'The Resistance having sonic weapons is very surprising, Emile. You're more advanced than we thought.'

Dr Emile Zante held his wife's hand as he spoke.

'What happened to you, Riz? As a child, you were the kindest person I knew and now....'

'I grew up, Emile. At least my parents saw my dedication to the Empire — yours will be turning in their graves to see what you've become.' He turned from the husband to the wife. 'I'd hoped to spare you all this, Zara, but you've left me no choice.'

She scowled at him. 'All you care about is yourself, Riz. And you've always wanted me for yourself. So you were happy for that mockery of a show trial – not because Emile helped those people, but because it meant you could finally get him out of the way. Isn't that true?'

The Butcher of Cassan wiped the blood from his lips. 'What about your unborn children, Zara?' He peered into the darkness behind us. 'It's a bit early to put them through the Ordeal of Kronos.'

Emile Zante gasped. 'How did you know about Zara's pregnancy?'

Orme's grin was as crooked as his brain. 'There are no secrets from the ruling elite, Emile. You know this.'

I stepped forward between husband and wife. And their unborn children.

'You knew Dr Zante was part of the Resistance?'

Orme's laugh cut through the gloom. 'You should never have come to this world, girl. Once we learn where your planet is, the Empire will ravage your people until nothing remains on your dead world.' He looked away from me and at the Zantes. 'We've known about your betrayal for years, Emile. I would have tortured and killed you long ago, but the Emperor said it was better to wait until we discovered the whereabouts of your other conspirators.'

I was glad he rambled as it gave me more time to think of a way out, but I didn't understand why he hadn't ordered his men to grab us. Or even shoot.

The metal against my throat irritated my flesh, and I cursed my luck for getting caught out with it. I slipped my hand into my pocket, found the control device, and pressed the screen without looking at it. I hoped it would unlock the prison around my neck with the sonic disruptor silent.

But it didn't. I needed more time.

'Did you enjoy slaughtering all those innocents on Cassan?' I said to him.

The gleam in his eyes was cold enough to make the hairs stand up along my arms.

'I did, child, very much so. Which is why I look forward to leading my men into a similar operation on your planet.'

I glanced at the swamp behind me. 'You'll have to catch me in there first, Orme. And I don't fancy your chances in the dark.'

He licked the blood from his lips as he grinned. 'We could take you now, you and the traitors, but I'd much rather wait until morning to see what remains of you in Kronos. Then the scientists will pick your body apart. After that, we'll discover the secret of your teleportation device and the location of your world. And if you're still alive by some miracle, I'll have some fun with you.'

I returned his grin. 'I look forward to it, Butcher.'

He stared at Emile. 'When you have to make the sacrifice in Kronos, Emile, will it be the alien child or the woman carrying your unborn children?'

Orme left those words hanging in the air, but neither he nor his men moved.

Emile whispered in my ear. 'Stay between Zara and me at all times.'

Then he led us into the swamp. And the darkness.

We stepped three yards inside, and they stopped, removing torches from their pockets. They switched them on, creating a bright light in front and behind us. Only then did I realise how vast the gloom was around us.

'How big is this swampland?' I said.

'Five miles ahead and on both sides,' Zara Zante said.

I rubbed my hands as an ice-cold wind swept across my face, glancing back to see more darkness. Orme and his men might as well have been on another planet instead of being just beyond the swamp's edge.

'I'll lead the way, then you and Zara behind me,' Emile said. 'Do you understand?'

I nodded. 'I'm guessing there's more danger here than just quicksand?'

He spoke as he moved slowly in front of us. 'This is Kronos. There are fifty such swamplands across Kaladan, and all have the same purpose.'

I kept one eye on his back and the other on the ground, careful where I stepped. So far, the earth had been hard underneath, but I knew from bitter experience how quickly an unfamiliar terrain could switch from safe to perilous.

'Why doesn't the Gleaming Planet terraform swamps like this? You have the technology for it.'

Zara answered the question. 'How much do you know of Kaladan and its people, Ruby?'

We moved at a snail's pace, and it would take hours to get across the swamp at this rate. But I didn't let my frustration get to me.

'I've visited Kaladan once before.' I couldn't tell them how their descendant, Zara, had saved me from certain death. 'So I studied some of the planet's history. I know all about the Royal Dynasty and the Kaladan Empire. Now, that Empire stretches across seven planets. That will triple in a hundred years.'

And it would be even greater five centuries from now, including Kaladan sending a conquering force to Earth.

Emile stopped walking, and we all followed suit. He didn't face me as he spoke, continuing to shine his torch into the surrounding darkness.

'You need to know something before we go further, Ruby.'

I shivered. 'Okay.'

'What you won't have learnt from your studies is the hidden history of this planet, one kept from its citizens apart from a select few.' Now he turned to me. 'We are not the indigenous species of Kaladan.'

A shriek cut through the air as Emile finished speaking. He spun on his heels, shining the light around us in a wide circle. Zara did the same, and I got a brief glimpse of our surroundings – it was nothing more than the swampland you'd find on any other planet.

But then that howl reappeared, followed by several others. So whatever it was, we weren't alone.

'We have to keep moving,' Emile said as he started walking.

'I'm guessing what we heard are the natives of Kaladan?' I said.

Emile shone the torch ahead of us. 'We call them the Yoron. They were here a hundred thousand years ago when our ancestors arrived, a primitive species that exists only to breed and feed. They walk on four legs, with a ferocious appetite, but they were no match for our technology.'

Suddenly, the darkness grew colder. 'So why didn't you wipe them all out?'

'Kaladanians live by only one rule,' Zara said, 'and that's the survival of the fittest. Do you know of it?'

'We have something similar on my world,' I said. 'But what's that got to do with having fifty swamps of these violent creatures on the Gleaming Planet?' The answer hit me before she could reply. 'You use these swamps as a test of strength for your people?'

She sighed, and I felt her breath on my neck. 'When we reach our teenage years, our elders send us in groups to face the Yoron. This is where Emile and I met during the Ordeal of Kronos.'

'And this isn't where we'll meet our end,' Emile said.

I pulled at the metal at my throat again. 'I could get us away if this wasn't hampering me.'

I removed the control device from my pocket and pressed it. But it was still a dud. Then the noises got closer.

'They won't come near the light,' Zara said. 'We just have to keep moving.'

And hope the torches didn't go out.

'How did you survive your ordeal?' I said.

Their silence only added to the strain running through me. The earth had grown wetter with each step. Now the damp seeped through my shoes and into my feet.

'There were twelve in the group,' Zara said behind me. 'All were approaching our thirteenth birthdays. We had no weapons, only the torches and our wits.'

'There are weapons on the ground if you look for them,' Emile said.

I glanced down, only finding mud and bits of stone.

'What type of weapons?'

He stopped, so we did, swinging his torch to the side and illuminating something large next to my feet. I bent to get it, wrapping my fingers around a bone as big as my arm.

Emile peered into my face. 'You can use that as a club.'

I was about to ask him what animal it was from until I realised what it was.

'This is from a Yoron?'

'Yes,' he said. 'They breed, and they eat. And if they can't capture a Kaladan child for food, they feast on the weakest of themselves.'

Great. Darkness surrounded us; hidden inside it were cannibal monsters desperate to kill and eat us. And I couldn't get the stupid restraint off my neck. Still, if groups of teenagers could survive this ordeal, why couldn't we?

The swamp crept further over my feet, like trudging through wet sand. The cold had increased to bite at my face, and everywhere smelt of rotten flesh. I put a hand to my nose and spoke.

'What's that stink?'

Emile swept the torch in front of him. 'We're getting close to the graveyard.'

I fought the urge to throw up, peering beyond him and into the moving light.

And then I saw them.

Bones. Piles of bones.

And bodies.

Carcases.

Zara dropped her voice to a whisper. 'We must find another way, Emile, to get around this.'

'No,' he said. 'It will take too long.' He turned to look at his wife. 'This is how we survived last time, so we'll do it again.'

'That was different, Emile. We have to go around.'

I stood between them as they stared at each other. And there was no light ahead of us. But still, I saw the things moving in the shadows. They walked on four legs, as large as horses, but with great teeth like sabre-tooth tigers and elephant-sized heads. Their eyes were burning yellow in the dark, at least six sets staring straight at me.

I clutched the blade, the handle digging into my skin as I scanned our surroundings, seeing Yoron corpses between the living beasts and us. Something had ripped the bodies open, with blood and entrails lying everywhere.

My legs didn't move as I spoke. 'If they feed on themselves, maybe they won't attack us.'

'No,' Emile said. 'That's not how the Yoron hunt. They'll return to the dead later, but now they'll descend as a pack on the weakest prey.'

'Please, Emile,' Zara said, 'don't do this again.'

I understood what she meant, speaking without taking my gaze from the Yoron.

'You sacrificed one of the others during your ordeal, didn't you, Emile?'

His voice trembled as he spoke. 'I'm sorry, Ruby; there's no other choice.'

Then he hit me in the head with the torch.

Chapter 4

Ruby's Diary

Day Seven Hundred and Eighty-Six, Year Three

Earth Time: Friday, 4 June 1976. Location: The Lesser Free Trade Hall, Manchester, UK. (Planet Earth).

When considering research into the history of anything, the single most unreliable thing is the human memory: except mine. My memory was near perfect apart from the missing first fourteen years of my life. I'd lost the greater part of my childhood, and now I'd lost my mentor and only friend.

'Don't come back, Ruby,' Diana had told me.

And I didn't.

So what was a young woman able to travel through all of time and space to do with her newfound freedom?

It was simple – enjoy myself.

The first thing I wanted was to experience life without having to observe it, to live it, not watch it, to be on the inside and not forever outside looking in.

That's why I went to Manchester in the blisteringly hot summer of 1976. Children were playing in parks, running through the sprinklers and laughing. Adults were sitting on park benches, reading newspapers and chatting with friends. I watched this happening around me, getting the occasional strange look for my long white hair and leather jacket.

The aroma of freshly cut grass and blooming flowers filled the air as I walked through the city centre, trying not to think of Diana and what had happened to her. The sunlight reflected off the Time Ring on my finger as I entered the cathedral. I made my way to a pew near the front and sat down. The noise of my beating heart and the distant chatter of tourists were the only sounds in the cavernous space.

I closed my eyes, letting my mind wander as I absorbed the tranquillity of the surroundings. The scent of incense and the cool air enveloped me, transporting me to a time before I was a fugitive on the run.

I spent the afternoon there, sitting alone and contemplating the things I'd done since escaping the Watchers. My life was one of flitting between places, never settling down, and not getting close to anybody. It seemed the best way to be.

In the evening, I visited another house of worship, somewhere that would acquire legendary status in the future. I clutched the paper in my hand. The date was misprinted as

1076, so I took that as a good omen. Buzzcocks were on the ticket as support, but a local heavy rock band, Solstice, replaced them. They entertained around thirty people in the audience, though you'd be hard-pushed to describe it as entertainment. Somebody near me said they were Bolton's third biggest rock band. Bolton had a lot to answer for.

But I wasn't there for them. Instead, I waited for four London lads, barely out of their teens, to play a bunch of 60s cover versions and a smattering of originals to a group of mutton-chopped hippies. I was there because I wanted to be part of history and observe it, to get involved with something that wasn't disasters, wars, or people dying. Though, by the look of the glum faces around me, it might have seemed like that for some of the audience. A tall, angular teenage boy peered at the stage through thick, dark glasses, clutching a notebook and pen. I glanced at the future superstar, and he turned away nervously.

After a torturous time that seemed to go on forever, the support band shuffled out of sight. I waited for the main event and scrutinised the surroundings, a small, strange, dull wooden auditorium with about two dozen people in seats. Nobody approached me or spoke to me, and I was happy about that. A conversation was the last thing I wanted.

I slipped into the shadows and propped myself against the wall. The venue smelt of cold beer and hot sweat, the aromas clutching at my throat. I tried not to think about what I'd do after the gig. Hunger gripped my stomach, but I ignored it, hoping the pain in my guts would override that in my head.

As I pressed against my belly, the band clattered on stage, swearing at the crowd as a few people bundled their way to the front. Some teenage girls gazed at the singer, who

31

stared at the audience, his eyes seemingly replaced with glaring red buttons from nuclear bombs. Those four lads I'd travelled in time to see looked like they were wearing clothes they'd slept in, jumble sale tops and trousers stolen from *Steptoe and Son*.

They ploughed into the music, playing as if they didn't care what anybody thought, especially those who'd paid to be there. I stayed in the shadows and watched the chaos unfold on stage, observing a rare jewel, a diamond in a field of tin. It was fast, energetic, and shambolic. The sound was dreadful, like having shit-covered screwdrivers forced into your ears, but best of all, it drowned out the noise that had followed me since Diana sent me away.

The music was magnificent. Freedom and rebellion rolled into one gigantic cacophonous coffin. Those around me stood wide-eyed and opened-mouthed. The young man with the paper and pen frantically scribbled into his book, trying to describe the indescribable. It was the youth I'd lost and the future I dreamed of. Not to be in a band or be a musician, but to grasp my life and, for the first time, live it as I wanted. Previous to my escape from the Watchers, I'd been an actor under somebody else's direction, but now I was free to take risks and make mistakes.

An electric charge shot through the room, and my blood turned hot in my veins. I stood there with the rest of the crowd; my limbs jerked around by invisible puppeteers. It seemed to last forever and be over in a whirlwind. There were two encores before it ended in a swirl of insults.

My third life had started, and I didn't know what I wanted.

But I knew I'd get it.

Chapter 5

The Shadows of Kaladan

I dropped the knife as I fell. There was just enough time to see it rolling away before the light of the torches disappeared. After that, the only illumination was from the moon and the gleaming yellow eyes of the beings a few feet from me.

The Yoron.

Then something smaller crawled towards me, small rat-like creatures with slathering teeth and burning red eyes. Two of the bravest ran toward my face, pouncing together as I grabbed the blade and slashed them in one long sweep.

They spilt their guts over my legs as I jumped up, their blood seeping into the swampland. Their hollowing cries and sliced bodies added to the smell of death surrounding me.

I kicked them away and waited for the next attack. Small animals like them shouldn't be any problem – it was the colossal Yoron I'd have issues with. I'd had to punch a cow back home on Earth once to get it off my foot, but these things were different.

But more rats ran at me, slower than the others, as if they'd watched and learnt from their dead brothers or sisters. They were slow enough it was easy to kick them away before they could cling to my legs. Yet it was still tiring, spinning to hit them from every direction. And the Yoron never moved, their great teeth glistening in the moonlight. By the time I'd finished fending the rats off, sweat had dripped off me even in the night chill.

And the restraint around my neck continued to irritate me like hell.

But it was the least of my worries.

The biggest Yoron broke away and marched toward me, its great legs thumping over the ground. Its eyes were blazing yellow, the teeth hanging over out of that vast mouth, preparing to snap me in half. I readied for the beast, hoping none of the others attacked me simultaneously. Instead, I scrutinised its approach, searching for a weakness to exploit.

I was still looking for it when the creature charged me.

The head was down, not facing me, the stink of its breath hitting me before it could. The shrieking of the other Yorons cracked the silence of the night; their howls, an animalistic death chant, aimed straight at me.

Before it reached me, I stepped aside like a matador,

spinning on my heels to see it stumble in the dirt. The force of its velocity created a giant wind that blew against me and nearly knocked me over. Then, as the Yoron struggled to turn back on me, I glanced at the rest of the creatures, expecting them to charge.

Yet they remained unmoved. If these were animals driven only by instinct, their behaviour was unusual. So I ignored them and focused on the beast that had attacked me. It charged again, but different this time. It appeared to anticipate my movement, following my faint to the side and catching me in the hip with its vast skull. Pain shot through me as I crashed sideways and into the dirt.

I jumped up as the beast hit me again, pushing me back as I tried to wrap my hands around its head. Its skin was like rugged leather, difficult to hold on to as it threw me into the rocks. I crumpled, expecting the force of the fall to dislodge the Time Ring attached to my spine. But instead, I rolled away, my face hitting the ground and swallowing dirt and grass.

The moon peered at me as I waited for the beast to rip my head off. After all this time searching for answers to the mysteries of my life – of meeting Diana and the Watchers, Daisy and Lucy, and even Gloriana and the Queens of Heaven – this was a strange way for me to end.

Those great legs thudded towards me, sending shock waves through my limbs. I dug my nails into the mud and tried to crawl away.

That's when I heard the voice. 'Get up, Ruby. You can't die like this.'

My vision blurred as I looked up. I searched for the Yoron or the owner of that female voice, finding nothing but the shimmering moon.

'Leave her; she doesn't deserve our help.'

That was a different female voice and another I didn't recognise.

Were the Yoron talking to me?

Was that even possible?

A shadow loomed over me as the first voice spoke again.

'Do you want to die here, Ruby, on this distant planet so far from your home?'

Before I could reply, one of the rat creatures ran over my foot, and I flinched back into the rocks.

My lips trembled. 'Who are you?'

'You know who we are, Ruby.' It was the second voice again. 'We're here to help you.'

More rats crept toward me, but I couldn't see who was talking. Perhaps it was all in my mind. Then the air shimmered in front of me, and a hand reached out. I took it, and she dragged me to her: Zara Zante.

'You came back?' I said.

'I'm sorry,' Emil Zante said. 'I made a mistake.'

I glanced from him to her. 'What about your unborn children?'

He grabbed me and I steadied my quivering legs. 'What kind of parents would we be if we'd left you here to die?'

I held their hands as I realised my Yoron attacker was approaching us.

'And now I've doomed us all,' I said.

I'd gone to Kaladan and sought Dr Zante to remove the device from my head, but now I wanted nothing more than Ishtar or any other Queen of Heaven to appear and rescue us.

I pushed myself in front of Zara Zante and readied for a fight I knew I couldn't win.

Until the revelation came that it wasn't a beast at all.

All three of you should follow me.

The Yoron spoke without speaking, its voice in my mind and I assumed, from their startled faces, of the Zantes. I stared at its massive head, scrutinising that grey leathery skin and yellow eyes to find signs of intelligent life but seeing nothing but a savage beast.

You must look not with your eyes, Ruby Quartz, but from what lies at the centre of you. Now come before the shacktie return in greater numbers to feast on you and the Kaladanians.

'Shacktie?' I said.

The shacktie are the animals you perceived to be rats.

They scuttled nearby, growing as a group.

Zara Zante fell to her knees. 'All those years ago, during the Ordeal of Kronos, I thought I was going mad when I heard the voices in my head.'

Her husband helped her up. 'It was the stress, my love, nothing more.'

She snapped her arm away from him. 'No, Emile. It was the Yoron; they spoke to me as they are now.'

Come below, and everything will become clear.

We looked at each other, shocked at what was happening, yet with little choice but to follow. The Yoron headed to the others of its kind, scattering the shacktie as its tree trunk legs stomped over the swampland. We followed in its wake, the Zantes holding hands as the illumination from their torches flickered close to empty.

Emile Zante whispered. 'We could flee; we might have enough light to escape.'

'You go if you want,' I said, 'but I need to discover what's happening here.'

The one who'd spoken in our minds led the others into a cave, and I stepped in behind them. I'd expected it to be in pitch darkness, but hundreds of glowing red stones in the walls illuminated the way.

Zara Zante touched one. 'I've never seen a mineral like this before.'

They are ancelorites, only existing deep below the surface of this planet.

The ground sloped, so we went down, the ancelorites providing heat and light. I glanced at Dr Zante, seeing the shock on his face and recognising his confusion. It was different for me; I was used to visiting other worlds and communicating with alien species. He and the rest of Kaladan had believed the Yoron to be mindless savage creatures for thousands of years.

And they clearly weren't.

After another minute of descent, the Yoron stopped, turning to us as I saw what was behind them: dozens more of their kind, including what could only be children and babies.

Emile Zante found his voice. 'How is any of this possible? The Yoron have hunted our offspring for generations?'

I felt the anger as the creature spoke.

No, man of Kaladan, your people arrived here generations ago and conquered this world. My ancestors spoke to yours in their minds, and the Kaladanians reacted with fear and hate. And violence. We have great strength in body and mind, but we were no match for your greater numbers and technology. So over time, all we could do was retreat to the swamplands and underground. But even then, your people used us for sport to teach your children how unfeeling you are as a species.

'What about the bodies we saw in the swamp?' I said.

You stumbled into a sacred ceremony of our dead.

'Why are you doing this?' I said.

All the Yoron looked at me, and when the voice came, I knew they were speaking as one.

You are different, Ruby Quartz. You are not of this world. You are not Kaladanian.

'How do you know that?'

That's because we see what's in your mind.

In that instant, I lost all thought of what we were doing and why I was on Kaladan.

'Can you see my missing memories? Do you know what happened to the first fourteen years of my life?'

Their sorrow seeped through me.

No, Ruby Quartz, we cannot see what was taken from you.

'Twenty years ago, I completed the Ordeal of Kronos,' Zara Zante said. 'Something spoke to me in my mind that day. Was it one of you?'

The silence cut through the cave as the ancelorites shone even brighter.

The old ones from that time are gone now. We are less with each passing year; our food sources are shrinking, and as the planet's temperature increases, it reduces the water in the swamps. So all the Yoron across Kaladan have prepared for our extinction. And then we sensed the human here tonight.

'Why am I important to you?' I said.

First, we must help you, Ruby Quartz.

None of the Yoron stirred as they spoke to us telepathically, but now they swayed together, moving slightly as if blown by a wind. Something shifted in the air, and all the hairs on my arms rose against my clothes. The ancelorites shimmered and glowed brighter as the material moved against my flesh. The temperature increased, and the restraint was warmer against my skin.

Then the metal pulled away from my neck and split

apart, falling to the ground with a thud. I put one hand to my throat, breathing correctly for the first time since the Butcher of Cassan had attached that infernal device to me. I reached for the trigger in my head, more in hope than anticipation.

And it was there.

Will you leave us, Ruby Quartz, and return to your planet?

A great part of me wanted to see Dash, Daisy, and Lucy. And then to find my missing friend, Diana.

But there was more I needed to know here. So I kicked the broken metal from me and walked to the Yoron.

'Tell me how I can help you.'

Chapter 6

The Resistance of Time

An echoing void settled around us as we waited for the Yoron to respond. The Zantes stood to the side, whispering to each other. Since the Yoron could read their minds, I assumed their behaviour was because of me. The doctor saw me scrutinising him, pulling his wife closer as if I was telepathic like our hosts. As I waited in silence, my thoughts returned to the last thing he'd said before the wall exploded in his house: he'd seen something unusual in my brain when removing the Kaladanian mind-connecting device.

'It was at the bottom of your cerebellum. It looked like part of it was burnt.'

It didn't sound like a natural occurrence from the way he'd said it. Had the damage been done when the Watchers removed my memories? Was Diana involved in it? I was about to ask him when his wife broke away and approached me.

'With everything that's happened, I still find it incredible that you're a time traveller, Ruby.'

I shrugged. 'It's one of many strange things in the universe.' I glanced at the Yoron. 'Some of which we've yet to discover.'

'Emile tells me you've travelled to our future and met a namesake of mine.'

I smiled at the memory of it. 'Yes, another Zara Zante. She saved my life.'

I couldn't tell her too much without risking more changes to my timeline. Or if I revealed important information about her descendant, would it change my future as well – something that was actually in my past now – so it would alter every subsequent thing I did, including me standing there with her?

Temporal paradoxes and time loops appeared to be everywhere.

'Was this during Kaladan's great democracy?' Emile Zante said.

The air chilled around me, and I took a deep breath. Since he'd operated on my brain, I hadn't looked forward to this part.

'I'm sorry, Dr Zante, but the Resistance will fail, and every time it tries again. In future, the Empire will have spread out from these seven planets to engulf several star systems, including mine.'

He gasped and stumbled back, resting his hand on the wall before sitting on a rock beside his leg.

'If you know all this, why haven't you done anything about it?'

'I might travel through space and time, Dr Zante, but I'm only one person. I have a friend who helps me, but there isn't much we can do against a star-spanning empire.'

Ever since I'd learned about humanity's disastrous encounter with Kaladan five hundred years from now, I'd wondered how I could prevent that from happening and curtailing the Kaladan Empire's ambitions. It had been one of the early time travel excursions Diana had taken me on, standing on this planet as the Earth ship landed.

'We only observe, Ruby. We never interfere as Watchers.'

How things had changed since then, apart from the continued growth of this terrible Empire through space and time. Now was my chance to stop it all – but how?

With our help, Ruby Quartz.

The Yoron spoke to me, but we all must have heard it. And Zara Zante had a question of her own.

'You never said why your ancestors contacted my mind twenty years ago in these swamplands.'

Over time, when your elders sent the children of Kaladan through our lands, we reached out to those we thought would be more sympathetic to our plight.

'What could a bunch of teenagers do for the troubles of the Yoron?' I said.

A small group can bring significant change if they have capabilities the majority don't. That's what my people have tried to achieve.

The magnitude of what they'd attempted hit me like a hammer.

43

'The Yoron are telepathic and telekinetic – you attempted to pass those abilities on to the Kaladanian children.'

Only some of them, the ones we thought would be sympathetic to our plight – those with empathy could share it with others, and those with great strength would utilise it in our struggle against the tyrants of this planet.

Zara Zante touched her head. 'But it didn't work. I have no special abilities.'

I gasped. 'It did work, only not as the Yoron intended.' I took Zara's hand in mine. 'Your descendant is telekinetic, one of only a few like that in the universe.' I looked at the Yoron. 'Your plan worked, but not in the generation whose brains you manipulated, but in the DNA of their descendants.'

Zara gripped my fingers. I peered into her eyes, wondering how she felt about what the Yoron had done to her. Then, finally, she let go of me and went to them.

'At first, when I heard the voices, I thought I was going mad, but later, I was calm. Then the Ordeal was over, and it felt like a gift had slipped away from me.'

Emile grunted. 'How will this help if the Resistance is fated to fail repeatedly?'

'This is different,' I said. 'Now I can focus on this one thing.' Dash, Diana, Watchers and Queens could wait. 'And we have the Yoron to aid us.'

Emile pushed up from the rocks and stared at our hosts.

'It's incredible what we've discovered here with the Yoron. It's a scientific wonder, but how will it help over-throw the Royal Dynasty and an Empire that spans seven planets?'

I had an idea, but first, I wanted more information from the Yoron and Dr Zante.

'We can't do anything about the other six planets yet. We must concentrate on Kaladan, the Gleaming Plane, at the Empire's centre. So tell me, Emile, how strong is the Resistance?'

He paused before answering, perhaps wondering if this was all some elaborate trick constructed by the Butcher of Cassan and the Empire to get his secrets from him.

'We are on every planet in the Empire, but our resources are focused on Kaladan.'

The way he emphasised the word *our* told me everything I needed to know about his determination. But he was about to become a father – how would that affect his conviction for a revolution?

'Are they enough to overthrow the ruling elite?'

He shook his head. 'Sadly, no. We have people inside all the branches of the military and the police. The other Resistance leaders and I are convinced that most who wear a uniform for the Empire would come to our side with the right motivation.'

'What type of motivation?'

'The biggest problem is Empress Isabella and the noble families. It's been impossible for the Resistance to get anybody close to them.'

The Kaladan Empire existed under a feudal system, with the Royal Family at the head. Then came the Lords and Ladies of the twelve noble families, followed by the landowners, and wealthy business owners, finally reaching the workers at the bottom. If you couldn't work for any reason – unless you were of the elite – you were of no use in the Empire, and slavery or death would follow. So I wasn't surprised the Resistance could not get anywhere near the top of the pyramid since those people had the most to lose. But they were vastly outnumbered by those at the bottom, even with the Empire's military strength. And at this point in history, it was at its weakest, as the Kaladan Empire had no off-world enemies.

'Do you think the Resistance could control the military and the police if you removed the Royal Dynasty?'

He nodded. 'With the people and resources we have in place right now, this might be the best chance the Resistance will ever get.' He glanced into my eyes before looking at his wife. 'Especially with what you told us about Kaladan's future.'

It was a start. 'What can you tell me about Empress Isabella?'

'She's the tenth ruler from the Krell dynasty,' Zara said. 'Five years ago, she ascended to the throne on her twenty-first birthday. Six months later, she married the eldest son of the noble Ryder family, Darius.'

'Do the noble families always marry between them?' I said.

'Yes,' Emile said. 'It keeps the twelve as the ruling elite.'

An idea was forming in my head. 'Has it been like this since your people came to this planet?'

'Yes, according to the history books. But many believe that is a lie, told through the years to keep the population in place. In school, we are taught that the noble families rule the rest of us because they have superior genetics.'

'A ruling bloodline, or bloodlines, running through the centuries,' I said.

'And, of course, it's all nonsense,' Dr Zante said. 'That so-called noble or royal blood is the same as yours or mine.' He looked at me and realised what he'd said. 'Well, different to yours, but not to any other person in their Empire.'

I smiled at him. 'As a doctor, have you tested the DNA of somebody from the nobles?'

'Yes, though I shouldn't have. My mentor, Dr Gartside, was the personal physician to Empress Isabella's father, the former Emperor Hurax III. It was a treasonous act, yet Dr Gartside smuggled blood and tissue samples from the Royal Palace back to his laboratory. We worked on them together, preparing a study that would shatter the myth of the noble bloodline.'

'What happened?'

The darkness in the cave slithered out of the shadows and crept over his face.

'He fell from the balcony of his home, fifty floors to the ground. His lab was closed, and I wasn't allowed back into it.'

'You believe somebody murdered him?'

'I try not to think about that awful night, but yes, I believe the Empire killed my friend.'

Zara touched her husband's arm. 'You never told me any of this, Emile.'

He wiped the darkness from his face. 'I had to keep it from you for your own safety, Zara.' He glanced beyond me at the Yoron standing there gazing at us. 'Though that seems redundant now.'

'Did the Empire know of your involvement?' I said.

'I didn't think so, but now I wonder if this was when they learned I was working with the Resistance. So they kept me under surveillance all this time until I broke their precious law not to help those who were starving.'

It made sense to me. 'If I could retrieve the data you and Dr Gartside discovered, would it be enough to get the people to rise against the Empress and the nobles?'

Zara answered. 'No, I don't think it will. We'll need more than that, something that reflects badly on Isabella.'

I noticed the glint in her eyes. 'And you have such a thing?'

'I might,' she said. 'Her husband, Darius, was a moderate in the ruling elite. The people loved him for his kindness and his speeches on reforming the Empire to benefit everybody.'

'Was?'

She sighed. 'He died three months ago, allegedly of natural causes in his sleep. He was twenty-six years old with no history of illness. So now the other families are busy presenting their errant children as Isabella's next husband. I don't doubt she will choose the most vicious and depraved of them. But even they wouldn't match the evil inside her.'

Zara's sadness touched my heart. 'Isabella rules with an iron fist?'

Emile Zante pulled his wife close to him. 'She's not that kind. Do you remember the Butcher of Cassan from my house?'

I rubbed at the mark on my throat. 'How could I forget?'

The lines had increased under Dr Zante's eyes. 'Cassan is a medium-sized city on the eastern continent of Kaladan. They were without food to feed everybody for two weeks, so some women marched through the streets in protest. It was only women and no men because the organisers thought that would prevent the Empire from squashing the demonstration with excessive force.' He shook his head. 'It was a major miscalculation of the evil inside Isabella. It was her idea to send in the troops, her order to kill all the women and each of their firstborn children. She announced this herself over a live telecast shown throughout the Empire. I know she travelled to Cassan to witness some executions.'

He glanced away from his wife. 'There are even rumours that she participated in the torture and murder. And she had it filmed to rewatch the suffering at her leisure.'

I clutched at my heart, trying to block the images in my head.

And then a voice pushed them out of my mind.

Now you know how to defeat the Empire of Kaladan.

Chapter 7

Stealing the Past

'If these videos exist of Empress Isabella torturing and killing her subjects, I can go back in time and steal them. Then all the Resistance must do is broadcast the clips across the Empire.'

Emile Zante shook his head. 'We'll need more than that, Ruby. The people will only rebel against the ruling elite if they think the military and the police won't massacre them.'

'You said you have Resistance people inside those groups.'

'We do, but they can only do so much without believing they have a chance of success.'

I understood what he meant. 'We must give them some hope before they take action.'

But what?

This is how the Yoron will help you.

I touched the bruise on my hip. 'Why did you attack me earlier?'

The great creature stepped away from the others and towards me.

We didn't know what you were then, Ruby Quartz. You were just another Kaladan child to be removed from our land until something in your brain spoke to me.

'In my brain? Didn't you read my mind?'

No – you contacted me first. That's when I stopped attacking you.

The mark on my throat started throbbing. 'I'm not telepathic.'

Perhaps it's something to do with your ability to travel through time and space.

'It's never happened before.'

Was there a connection between it and having the Time Ring fused to my spine?

Emile approached me. 'How can the Yoron help the Resistance achieve a people's revolution?'

Ruby Quartz knows the answer.

'Do I?'

Did I?

Zara touched my arm. 'I think you do.'

I gazed at the Yoron and guessed I did. 'You'll support the revolt against the Empire?'

Across the planet, our numbers are only a few thousand. If we don't do this now, there will be no Yoron left soon.

I turned to Emile. 'How many military bases and police stations would the Resistance need to control before you could get the population's support?'

'In the capital, a dozen each. Across the planet, we'd have to take over every city controlled by the other noble families. But we've always known this and have people and weapons in place – we must take out the most strategic points.' He thought for a second. 'Over those twelve locations, it would be between one hundred and fifty and two hundred sites. But we don't have enough people to take control from the authorities.'

We'd need a minimum of two hundred buildings to wrest control from the Kaladan Empire to kick start a revolution. Could we do that? I moved closer to the Yoron and stretched my mind into theirs.

And they agreed to my plan unconditionally.

* * *

I took the Zantes fifty miles from the swampland into a Resistance safe house. Emile's colleagues and friends were overjoyed to see them. They were a mixture of ages, but I was surprised by how many looked so young. They stared at me with curiosity as Emile and Zara revealed what had happened in the swamplands. On hearing this, some of the younger ones muttered amongst themselves, and I heard more than one saying how they'd felt something in their minds during their Ordeal. Then I retired to a bedroom to rest, unable to remember the last time I'd slept without being knocked on the head. I left it to Emile to explain who I was.

* * *

I woke six hours later, refreshed and counting the new bruises on my body as I wondered what Dash would say when she saw them.

Dash. I considered returning to Earth for her help. It was tempting, and I missed her, but I couldn't get her involved in a revolution that might go horribly wrong. Plus, I didn't want to leave Daisy and Lucy alone again in the base. So it was up to me, the Resistance and the Yoron to make it work. And the ordinary people of Kaladan, once we gave them a cause to fight for.

I gathered my thoughts before joining the others, knowing there was something I needed to do before speaking to my new partners. So I flicked the trigger in my brain and disappeared. Four minutes later, I returned and stepped into the main room.

Emile Zante handed me a glass of water. 'The Resistance plans are in motion.'

I sipped from it. 'You found enough vehicles?'

He nodded. 'More than enough.' He glanced at his colleagues busying themselves in the other room. Zara was resting upstairs. 'The biggest challenge was convincing people to work with our new friends. But we did. Every Resistance member knows we are on the cusp of history.' Or we were all on the precipice of disaster.

A few of his folk studied me through disbelieving eyes and ridiculed the idea of time travel, though not to my face. Still, everything seemed possible once people adjusted to the notion that the Yoron were intelligent creatures and telepathic.

I shook his hand. 'It's time for me to go.'

'You've memorised the details and the locations?'

'I went through it all before I slept. Doing it then helps the information cement into my brain.' I'd learnt that with

53

Diana. She'd always teach me the most critical things shortly before I slept. 'I'll start inside the Royal Palace. Then, when I've got the videos, I'll return here and give them to your people for broadcast. Then I'll move on to the next stage.'

Dr Emile Zante smiled at me. 'Best of luck, Ruby Quartz.'

I thought of the location provided by the Resistance and found the trigger in my head. All the eyes in the room were on me, including those who thought I was a liar.

Then I vanished.

I reappeared in the gloom, standing in the shadows inside the Royal bedroom. When discussing the plan with Emile, the initial idea was for me to go back in time and steal the clips not long after their creation. Then Zara thought that stealing the videos so early would only alarm Empress Isabella's security and likely put them on heightened alert weeks before our prime attack. So we decided to retrieve them thirty minutes before the main assault on the forces of the Empire.

There were no windows in the room; the only illumination came from dozens of candles. That helped me linger in the shadows near the occupied bed. It was the middle of the afternoon, always a good time to start a revolution, but our information was that Isabella always took a nap then. Unfortunately, none of the Resistance spies could discover where the Empress kept the incriminating videos, so we had to develop another way to get them.

'I'll make her tell me where they are,' I said.

Apart from Emile Zante, the whole table stared at me with incredulous eyes.

'How?' one of the youngest fighters said. 'Isabella has a

heart of stone. So you won't be able to torture the information out of her.'

So I told them what I'd do. And now I was in that Royal bedroom to do it.

I removed the gun from my jacket and scanned the room, finding it empty, apart from me and the person in the bed. I crept forward, pulled back the cover, and pointed the pistol at the sleeper.

Dead eyes peered at me.

The young man was of indiscriminate age, the blood covering his face making him hard to describe. There were cuts across his chest, leading to his groin. The smell was fresh, his death recent. I'd seen dead bodies before, but this was different. The killer had taken their time and enjoyed it.

'I call it my afternoon delight.'

Empress Isabella Vale stepped towards the other side of the bed, dressed in a long silk silver gown. She had Marilyn Monroe's eyes and Medusa's smile. There was a drink in one hand and a blood-red blade in the other.

I waved the gun at her. 'You do this every day?'

'Well, a girl has to get her pleasures somehow. What about you, mysterious stranger?'

I looked away from the body. 'What will your people think when they learn of this?'

She ran her tongue around the top of the glass. 'Why would anybody discover this? Nobody leaves this room alive without my permission, including you.'

'I'll press this gun to your head and take you hostage. Your security will let me out.'

Isabella grinned, highlighting the glint of red in her teeth.

'Unless that weapon is a hundred years old, it won't

function.' She pointed the blade at the ceiling. 'Only natural things work in here.' She put the knife to her lips and licked the blood from it. 'Now, it might be interesting if you had one of these.'

'Don't you want to know how I got past your security?'

She shrugged. 'It doesn't matter. You can't get out before I gut you with this blade.'

The Empress was as disturbed as they said, and there was no need to waste more time.

'I'm not going anywhere if you think you can take me, Isabella.'

She finished her drink and threw it behind her. 'You'll suffer even more for that insult, girl. You address me as Your Majesty.'

I shook my head. 'That will all be redundant if a few hours when your Empire is no more.'

She gripped the knife and jumped at me.

And the Empress was quicker than she looked.

Isabella hit me in the shoulder with her fist, my gun blocking the blade before it pierced my stomach. Our weapons tumbled to the floor, bouncing into the wall as she wrestled with me. She dug her nails into my arm, and I was glad.

Now she was stuck to me.

I flicked the trigger in my brain, and we vanished from the Royal bedroom.

We landed on the other side of the universe three thousand years ago. I hit the ground first, Isabella clinging to me as we rolled over. The shock of the journey loosened her grip on me, and she let go. I bounced up before she did, the midday sun striking my face as I readied for Isabella's next attack. But, as she stood, she was too busy gazing at our surroundings to worry about me.

'What.... what sorcery is this?'

I wiped the dust from my clothes. 'I didn't realise the technocrats of Kaladan believed in magic.'

She ignored me and gazed at the great stone structures nearby. 'Where are we?'

'This is my planet, and that's Stonehenge.'

Isabella stood motionless near the stones as we watched the long procession marching towards the middle of the inner circle. There must have been more than a hundred in the group, with those at the front using ropes and cloth to transport bodies wrapped in dark covers.

'This isn't possible,' Isabella said as the funeral march continued.

'What, that people would treat the dead with respect? Or even the living?'

The wind blew the hair from her face, giving the Empress the appearance of a wild animal. The fire burned in her eyes as she snarled at me.

'You've drugged me somehow; this is all an illusion.' She inched closer to me. 'What is your name?'

'Well, Your Majesty, you can call me Ruby.'

She struggled to keep her arms steady at her sides. 'What do you want?'

'You need to give me the contents of your video collection – the one with you torturing and killing people.'

I expected her to snarl at me again, but she let out a tremendous howling laugh instead. Some of the funeral procession glanced our way, but thankfully, none broke off to confront us.

'Are you a connoisseur like me, Ruby?'

'Yeah, I need them for my collection. So where do you keep them?'

Isabella peered into the sky, staring at the birds hovering above.

'Why should I do anything for you?' She showed me her hands as if waiting for a tribute. 'You used technology to transport me here. That's impressive, but it doesn't inspire me to help you.' She grinned at me. 'Are you going to threaten to leave me here? Because I quite like the idea of starting afresh somewhere else.' She was only a few feet from me. 'Those idiots in the noble families think that like my father before me, it's the power of Empire I seek. But it's not. My pleasure comes from inflicting pain on others, and I can do that anywhere.' She scrutinised the funeral procession as they reached the inner circle of the stones. 'This looks like the perfect place for me to live. It was so restraining living inside the bubble of privilege, hating everybody around you, including all those mindless, filthy peasants who call themselves my subjects. But this world could be the answer to all of my dreams.'

'You enjoy torturing and killing people?'

Isabella put a finger in her mouth and rubbed it along her lips. When she removed it, blood covered her skin.

'Enjoy it? I love it – it was what I was born to do. My father recognised it in me early on, perhaps when I was five or six, and instead of being horrified at his only daughter, he nurtured that desire in me. And then we spent a glorious time together as parent and child as he trained me.'

'Trained you to do what?'

'To kill, of course. So he started me on some of the street children who lived rough in the city. He thought it would be better if they were near my age at the beginning. I'm not sure if that was important, but I can't deny I get more enjoyment from strangling a six-year-old than an older person.' A nostalgic look overtook her face. 'I'm looking forward to

killing you, but nothing will ever repeat the exquisite pleasure I got with my favourite kill.'

I was afraid to ask, but I did. 'You murdered a baby?'

Isabella put a hand to her chest and laughed. 'Slaughtering a child is more like the first course of your meal, and
I'm talking about a main course that can never be repeated.'

'You're ill.'

'Perhaps, but haven't you guessed who I'm talking
about?'

That's when I saw it in her eyes. 'You assassinated your
mother?'

'Of course I did.' She showed me her palms. 'I strangled
her with these hands and recorded everything. Once my
father died, there was no need to keep her around.'

'And your husband?'

She stuck out her cheeks like a child. 'He had to go as
well. Once the marriage cemented the bond between the
noble houses and we pacified the moronic population by
having him at my side, it was only a matter of choosing the
right moment to dispense with him. I'll give him some credit
– at least he didn't whimper or scream like the others, especially when I plucked out his eyes.'

'I don't have to leave you here, Isabella; I can take you to
any terrible spot in the universe.'

When the laughter burst out of her, it nearly blew me
over.

'Fine, do your worst. Do you think I fear any place you
might leave me?'

No, I knew she didn't. So I stepped forward and
punched her in the face. She fell back and hit the ground.
Pain rippled through my knuckles, but it was worth it. I
removed the clips from my pockets and restrained her hands
and feet. The funeral procession continued in the distance,

with nobody looking our way. Once I'd finished with the rest of the plan, I'd return in four minutes to haul her back to Kaladan.

And if any locals wanted to poke her with a stick while I was away, I was fine with that.

Chapter 8

The Revolution of Time

I reappeared at the Resistance safe house to gasps and a
few with fear in their eyes. I'd seen that look before
when appearing out of nothing in front of people.

'Did you get the video?' Emile Zante said.

'Not quite.' I reached into my jacket and removed the
micro-camera with an internal hard drive. 'She would never
give me those incriminating clips no matter what I did, but
this should do.'

I handed him the equipment. 'What is this, Ruby?'

'Before I went to the palace, I borrowed the camera from your old house, Emile. I hope you don't mind?'

He peered at the device. 'You recorded your conversation with Empress Isabella?'

'I did. I think you and the Empire will find it illuminating.'

So I gave them a rundown of what she'd told me, and there were more gasps in the room.

'I knew she was evil,' Zara said, 'but to do those things, to murder babies and her own mother and husband, is beyond belief.'

'Let's hope the rest of the Empire believes it and the people rise against it.' I turned to her husband. 'Is everything still on time?'

He looked at his watch. 'All the trucks are in place, just waiting for the signal.' He clutched the camera. 'I'll get this to the technicians, and it should be ready for transmission across all channels soon.'

'Good. And you're sure your people can hack into the State media and replace it with that video?'

Emile smiled at me. 'They're already in the system. The Empire is so lax in their media security they've become overconfident.'

I nodded. 'Broadcast it in ten minutes. That's the signal to alert those in the trucks.'

Before he could reply, I vanished.

We were in the last stage now.

I landed outside the cave in the swamplands. The ground was empty, the Yoron waiting below for my arrival. The air chilled my skin as I took a deep breath. Then the woman stepped out of the shadows, raising her arm so I could see the scars on her hand.

'You don't have to do this, Ruby.' It was the last thing I needed.

'You have me at a disadvantage, stranger. You never introduced yourself when we met in that hospital room.'

'Who I am isn't important – it's what I represent you should respect.'

I laughed in the gloom. 'The Watchers? The mighty observers who sit on the sidelines while millions die and planets are ravaged and subjected.'

'It's the natural order of things. You and the others have no right to change time – to alter history.'

'And what right do you and the Watchers have to tell me what to do?' I showed her my wrists. 'You experimented on other children and me. None of you gets to tell me what to do.'

'The Watchers didn't experiment on you or anybody else, Ruby; that was the Queens of Heaven.'

One of those rat-like creatures ran between us.

'Semantics. The Queens are a faction in the Watchers, but you're all the same to me.'

'If you do this, Ruby, the consequences will ripple forward for centuries.'

'Yes, I know – and all those consequences will be good.'

She shook her head. 'Do you know what is supposed to happen today?'

'Something terrible?'

'This is the day the Yoron rise against their oppressors. Across the planet, they leave the swamplands and march peacefully into the nearest Kaladan city, where the authorities kill them all.'

'And you want that to take place?'

'It is the natural order of things.'

'You keep saying that, but I don't believe it means what you think it does.'

'One day, Ruby, your blasphemy will catch up with you, and you'll understand I was right all along.'

She disappeared with those words, leaving me wondering how many more times a Watcher would lecture me before they gave up.

Is it time, Ruby?

I turned to see the Yoron behind me, over thirty of them staring at me.

'Did you hear another mind up here with me?'

No, only you.

Perhaps the scarred Watcher left before they could sense her presence. But it didn't matter as there were more important things for us to do.

'Are you all ready?'

We've been ready all our lives.

As had I. I reached into my memory, retrieving the data for the locations of the military and police buildings the Resistance needed to secure the city. Then I found the coordinates for the rest of the planet's Yoron swamplands, all fifty of them.

'Your community know what I'm about to do?'

We are ready, Ruby Quartz.

I touched her side. Then I flicked the trigger and took us to the police station closest to the Royal Palace. As we landed inside the largest room, officers stood with shocked faces staring at the screen showing the video I'd taken of Isabella's conversation with me. Before they could react, the Yoron reached into all their minds and sent them to sleep.

'I can leave you to do the rest of them in the building?'

Go, Ruby – finish what you've started.

So I did, travelling to every Yoron community and

taking one individual to all the significant Empire security facilities in the city. At the same time, Dr Zante and the Resistance had organised their people to transport the Yoron in trucks to most of the military and police buildings in every major city and town. The Yoron would send as many soldiers and officers to sleep while the Resistance organised the population to revolt and take over.

After completing my part with the Yoron, I returned to Stonehenge and the Empress. I arrived as she studied the ceremony inside the stones. Fatigue possessed every inch of me, but an adrenaline rush kept me going.

Isabella twisted her head and glared at me. 'I look forward to torturing you for weeks on end.'

I ignored her and watched as people placed mementoes on the burial site. I observed their displays of grief, love and respect, giving myself a moment to breathe. Then I grabbed Her Royal Highness, Empress Isabella Vale, and returned her to Kaladan. She was still cursing when I dropped her at the feet of Zara Zante and the rest of the Resistance.

Most of them gasped when they saw her. Isabella stood to see where she was and who she was with.

'I'll have you all killed for this.'

I pulled Emile to the side. 'How is it going?'

He beamed at me. 'The outrage over the video has spread across the Empire like wildfire. It was enough to instigate a massive uprising with our prompting.'

'And the Yoron?'

'It's been all good news so far. Soldiers and police officers have deserted in droves to come to our side. The revolution is succeeding, Ruby.'

I slumped in a chair and watched the realisation drift across Isabella's face. So many time jumps in quick succession were exhausting, but at least I hadn't visited the same place twice too close together – that would have put me on the floor with the Empress and in much worse pain.

She scowled as two women restrained her. 'You think this pitiful rebellion will bring down an Empire? You're more foolish than you look.'

'Can you lock her somewhere, so we won't hear her whining?' I said.

'Shouldn't we get her in front of a camera to show the people of Kaladan and the Empire she's our prisoner?' Emile said.

I shook my head. 'We'll save that until we know. We don't want to give any of her fanatics the excuse to come looking for her.' I thought of the Butcher of Cassan and wondered where he was.

The women dragged Isabella away as I scanned my surroundings. Dr Zante and the others had constructed a bank of computers and screens throughout the house, and they were all showing the same thing: Isabella's conversations with me in the royal bedroom and at Stonehenge. The response from the public was overwhelmingly negative towards her and the Empire and encouraging for us. Some claimed the clips as fraudulent, but they were in the minority.

Zara sat next to me and handed me a small screen. 'This is a sample of what's happening around the Empire.'

People had gathered in the street, calling for the Empress's removal and the Empire's dismantling. And it was heartening to see how many uniformed soldiers and police officers were joining them with no signs of violence.

I returned the device to her. 'This is going better than we thought.'

She nodded. 'There are pockets of opposition, but they are mainly focused on the houses of the noble families.'

I sat up straight. 'I could do something about that.'

Zara took my hand. 'You should rest, Ruby. Our people will deal with the nobles.'

She was right. I needed half an hour before starting the next step of retrieving the Yoron from where I'd left them. I hoped none of them had been hurt. So I stayed with Zara, watching the revolution unfold in real time. There was little news from the other planets in the Empire, but Kaladan was the focus, especially the capital. Once that fell to Resistance control, it would send a powerful message to the rest of the planet. And the Empire.

At some point, I closed my eyes and drifted off. Not quite asleep, but I wasn't fully awake either. Zara left me to join her husband, and I could still hear the noise around me. I would have sworn I heard Isabella shouting from upstairs at one stage until I realised I was remembering our conversation at Stonehenge.

Stonehenge. It made me think of Dash. This was the first adventure I'd undertaken without her since I'd saved Dash from Felineous several lifetimes ago. Of course, when I returned to the base and told her about this, she would be furious. But I had to admit that the Kaladanian revolution had been just the distraction I'd needed from all my other problems, as flippant as it sounded.

And now that the mind-communicating device was out of my head, I wouldn't have to worry about Ishtar or any other Queens of Heaven invading my thoughts. Yet, that mechanism had come from Kaladan, acquired by Dash from a person unknown. And Dr Zante had claimed the technocrats of the Royal Court manufactured it. So, had Dash stolen it from them, or had she dealt directly with Isabella and her scientists?

I pondered that question when Zara shook me awake.

She beamed at me as I opened my eyes. 'You don't want to miss this, Ruby.'

A computer was on her lap, with the screen split into four.

I rubbed at my face. 'What am I watching?'

Her grin warmed my heart. 'The collapse of the noble families.'

Groups gathered outside grand, luxurious buildings on each display, cheering as uniformed police officers led unhappy-looking nobility handcuffed into the streets.

'This is the end, Ruby,' Emile said. 'And it's all thanks to you.'

I squeezed the last of the lethargy from my body and stood.

'No, Emile. None of this would have been possible without you, Zara, the rest of the Resistance, and the people of Kaladan. And the Yoron.'

Now I had to return them to their communities. I disappeared from the group and revisited all the places I'd left the Yoron. I spent longer returning them to their homes than on the first journeys, ensuring they were okay and talking to them about what had happened with the soldiers and police officers. Of the fifty-two Yoron I transported through space, only three had encountered difficulties, none of which had been life-threatening. Though I knew they lived and worked as a collective, the one I perceived as the leader at the Kronos swamplands was the last to accompany me on the trip back.

The community was waiting for her when we returned.

'What happens now?' I said.

After today we will have a greater connection with the people of Kaladan – and a greater understanding of each other. This is a fresh beginning for all of us. And what is next for you, Ruby Quartz?

I glanced into the Kaladanian sky before smiling at my new friends.

'Now I have to discover what happened to my past.'

Chapter 9

Ruby's Diary

Day Eight Hundred, Year Three

Earth Time: 2232. Location: Kostuk. (Planet Pegula).
Everything was grey on Pegula, from the sky to the sand. It was harsh and unwelcoming, the perfect place to get my head right. I planned for a three-month stay but was open to something longer. After all, I was free, and there was no rush to go anywhere.

However, I didn't intend it to be a vacation. Instead, I wanted to do something different, the opposite of what I'd done since my parents handed me over to Diana. That had been constant learning, travelling, and observing, with the occasional fraught adventure. Now I needed peace, quiet and monotony, so I avoided all the places I could have gone for an idyllic holiday.

Kostuk was Pegula's capital, a place similar to twenty-first-century Earth, with comparable technology. But, unlike Earth, a single system ruled Pegula across its five continents. It was rigid and authoritarian, yet it was simple for me to create digital records under a false identity, set up a job, and get a flat on a modern housing estate. It would be the first time I'd lived within a community, and the prospect excited me.

The office was a maze of outdated equipment and cluttered desks, with dust covering everything. The air was thick with the hum of malfunctioning machinery and the chatter of stressed employees. I made my way through the cramped aisles to find my station. My co-workers were hunched over their work, typing away at clunky computers, surrounded by towering stacks of paperwork. It seemed like they were all fighting a losing battle against the overwhelming amount of information that had to be processed. Yet, it was exactly what I needed.

Nobody spoke to me the whole day, even during the short breaks allowed for food or a visit to the toilet. The work was monotonous, inputting demographic data of the city's population. However, it gave me an idea of the make-up of Kostuk. At the end of the shift, I used the public shuttle system to return to my flat. The living room was minimalistic, with a sleek white sofa and a glass coffee table as the focal point. A large TV was mounted on one wall, but the rest were empty. I preferred it that way, able to stare into a blank space and gather my thoughts.

That's how it went until my neighbour invited me to an estate party. The residents were busy setting up tables with food and drink as the smell of cooked meat drifted in the air. Groups of children ran around bursting balloons and using the makeshift swimming pool at the end of the street. I stood and watched, observing again, wondering if any of my childhood had been like this.

'I'm Elizabeth,' my neighbour said as she gave me a warm smile. 'And this is my husband, Charles.'

They appeared to be in their early sixties, her with long grey hair and him looking anxious and on edge. I told her my fake history, though I kept Ruby as my name. He went off to get a drink while she chatted with me. The longer she spoke, the more I recognised the stress behind her eyes.

'Are you okay?' I said.

She took a deep sigh and finished her wine. 'It's Charles. There's something wrong with his memory.'

He'd disappeared amongst a group of children, but she hadn't noticed.

'Memories?'

Elizabeth touched my arm, and I got the distinct impression she was desperate for somebody to talk to.

'He's ill; I know that. It started a few years ago, with him forgetting simple things, but it's worse now. And I can't pay to take him to a doctor. Not that I trust a government one, anyway.'

Pegula was not a planet that protected its most vulnerable citizens, not if they couldn't afford it. I'd realised that by studying the data I processed at work. It wasn't strictly the survival of the fittest, but it was hardly a society that looked after its most vulnerable.

Her hand trembled as I squeezed it. 'Is there anybody to help you?'

Elizabeth shook her head. 'No, we're all we have.' She glanced nervously around at those enjoying themselves. 'I don't have any friends here. Most folk keep to themselves, so I was surprised when somebody organised this.' She smiled at me. 'And it's so nice to meet new people.'

A sound above me drew my attention to the sky, peering at a drone moving over the party.

'A neighbour?' I said.

'More likely the State is spying on us again.' She moved closer to me. 'I work part time at the post office, and rumours are going around about some big new government initiative dealing with so-called "undesirables".

'Undesirables?'

'Anybody who doesn't contribute to the State.'

As I considered her words, somebody screamed from the direction of the swimming pool. Elizabeth let go of me and sprinted towards the commotion. So I followed.

When I got there, Charles was submerged in the water, throwing toy ducks into the air and blowing cigarette smoke into the faces of the kids. They shrieked as the adults ran to the overflowing pink plastic and dragged Charles from the pool. The fact he was naked didn't help. Elizabeth took him from them, cringing at the barrage of insults directed at her. And all the while, the drone hovered above them.

I helped her take him home and inside. She led him upstairs to get dry and fresh clothes. I left her to it and went to the window, peering through the blinds at those scowling and pointing at the flat. The drone was still nearby.

Elizabeth returned five minutes later, looking as if she wanted to disappear into a black hole.

'Is he okay?' I said.

She slumped onto a sofa, and I sat opposite her. 'Can you imagine your life was stolen from you, Ruby? Each moment scooped from your brain like an industrial digger, cutting into your mind and dumping all your personality and memories into a recycle bin beyond your grasp. Yet, somewhere out of sight, in the shadows of your skull, there are phantoms of people and places you used to know.' I listened as she put her face in her hands. 'God forgive me, but I wished he'd got cancer or some other fatal disease instead of this. At least if it was that we could talk and laugh together, remember all the good times we'd had during such a happy marriage. There's no love, no sharing, and no togetherness with this.'

'I can get you both to a doctor, Elizabeth, somebody not State-sanctioned.' The information was already in my head, transferred from the data I saw at work. 'They might help.'

'That's kind of you, Ruby, but we can't afford it.'

'I'll pay, Elizabeth. It's no problem.'

I thought she'd protest, but instead, she reached over and grabbed my hand, the tears slipping down her cheek.

'Thank you, Ruby. I've only just met you, yet you've done more for me than anybody else. You've done more for us.'

I sat with her for a while, the flat silent apart from the slow rumble of snoring from upstairs. Then, when I returned to my flat and stared at the wall between us, I knew why I'd chosen that planet.

Chapter 10

Nagasaki Nightmare

D ash, Daisy and Lucy were sitting around the table eating when I returned, the room smelling of grilled fish, roasted vegetables and some unknown spice. My stomach grumbled as soon as I appeared, and I remembered I hadn't eaten in a while. I rubbed at the mark Dr Zante had left on me from the operation.

'Ohhhh,' Daisy said as she stared at the wound on my head. 'Does it hurt?'

'It won't if you don't touch it.'

She lunged towards me, trying to poke at the scar. I

picked her up and spun her around the room. She squirmed out of my grasp and ran in a circle, pretending to be King Kong. Watching her burn up so much energy made my bones ache even more than they already did.

'Were there any problems?' Dash approached me with a drink, but I refused it. Should I tell her of the rebellion I'd started on Kaladan? And ask her who she'd dealt with on her last visit to that planet. It might have been wise to leave that until later, but I had promised no more secrets between us.

Daisy ran out of energy and sat next to her mother while I gave them all the brief highlights of my excursion to Kaladan.

'Wow,' Lucy Lynx said. 'You're a revolutionary, Ruby.'

I smiled at her while Dash glared at me.

'Why did you do something so risky on your own?'

Daisy replied before I could. 'The bad people have to be stopped, Dash. I know that from history.'

There was no arguing with that, even from Dash. Instead, she silently judged me as I ate, finishing two plates while Daisy and her mother played cards in the corner. Then Dash spoke.

'So, what now?'

I dragged a chair in front of a computer. My questions for Dash about who she'd contacted on Kaladan could wait: it was time to save my friend.

'We need to find Diana.'

Dash grabbed a seat next to me. 'You've thought of a strategy?'

I pulled up the plans of the Nagasaki Medical School and Hospital on the screen.

'We must arrive outside the building five seconds before

the bomb drops and be inside as it explodes. After that, the loop starts, and the guards won't be able to follow us inside.'

'No hopping straight into the building?'

I shook my head. 'There's no telling who will be there when we appear.'

'Why don't you hide somewhere in the hospital beforehand, say a week before?' Lucy asked. I wished it could be that simple.

'The Queens will have cleared and checked the building every day until the point of impact. So as soon as we get inside, they'll know we're there. It may be 1945, but they'll litter the hospital with futuristic hi-tech equipment, including cameras everywhere. We must disable those along with any security we encounter. The hospital has three floors plus a basement, which seems the likeliest place to conduct large-scale experiments since it contains a storage area and a morgue.'

Dash looked at me. 'What's the plan when we get there?'

'Search, destroy and grab. Just like the old days.'

'How will you get out?' Lucy said. 'If the atomic explosion keeps your friend from escaping, how will you do it?'

It was a good question I didn't know the answer to. Not yet, anyway.

'They must have an exit. They wouldn't lock themselves in the loop without a way out. So Dash will charm it out of them.'

We smiled at each other, and I ignored my guilt about keeping more secrets and not telling her what Dr Zante had said about my cerebellum. It was probably meaningless, something unique to me, and we had to stay focused. I couldn't have her worrying about my brain again.

Dash patted Daisy on the hand. 'It's time for another of our grand adventures.'

The kid and her mother watched as we prepared for the journey, getting the weapons and tech we needed.

'Don't you want to rest before we go?' Dash said. 'After all, you've just come from bringing down an Empire?'

Had we succeeded in our revolution? I could nip into the future to check, but was reluctant to do so. If the whole thing had failed, I didn't want that disappointment weighing me down as we tried to rescue Diana.

'Now's the best time since I'm still pumped full of adrenaline from the events on Kaladan.'

She scrutinised me, not totally convinced by my words. 'Okay, then.'

'Are we ready?' I made sure I had everything I needed in my pockets. Dash nodded, and we took turns hugging Daisy and Lucy. 'We'll be back soon.' I hoped it was true.

Then we vanished together.

I arrived first. Two guards snapped to attention, thrusting swords in my direction; only they weren't swords, as they bristled with electricity. They wore the uniforms of the Japanese military, with red caps adorned with a brass five-point star. They were the Imperial Guard working for the Queens of Heaven, armed with weapons designed hundreds of years after their deaths. Before they attacked, they dropped to the floor.

'That was perfect timing.' Dash blew across the barrel of the stun gun in her hand.

I didn't hesitate, barging through the entrance to the hospital. Dash was right behind me as we stormed into the security on the other side. My head hit a padded shoulder, sending both of us down. As I landed on top of the guard, she struggled to reach the handgun strapped to her side. I wedged my elbow under her chin, mesmerised by the scar running across her throat. Was that why she was silent? The hairs on my arms sprang to attention as something roared outside the building, and the concrete vibrated around us.

'Watch out!' Dash shouted as I pushed my weight into the woman floundering beneath me. The burst of the laser flashed past my cheek, hitting a body above me. She fired again, high into the walls, sparks flying as I squeezed my assailant unconscious. As I leapt to my feet, the thunderous sound of more people heading our way helped me decide which way to go.

'Basement.'

I pointed to the stairs at the end of the corridor. A group of armed Japanese women came around the corner, so I lobbed two canisters of immobilising gas at them. Dash and I wore hidden air filters in our nostrils. The guards froze on the spot like victims of Medusa.

'That will keep them quiet for an hour.' I headed for the exit to the basement.

'Shame we haven't got any more of that stuff,' Dash said as the door closed behind us.

I had my weapon pointed forward as we crept down the stairs and my shoulder pushed into the wall. The stairwell was camera free, silent apart from our descent. I grasped the trigger in my mind, trying to squeeze a hop into the space below us, but nothing happened. Instead, pain seared through the front of my head. Dash must have had the same idea, as her face bristled with frustration.

'The theory about the bomb turns out to be true. No matter how hard I push my mind, I can't go anywhere.'

There was anxiety in her voice, probably because she was thinking again about how we would escape. I concentrated on finding Diana, ignoring my guilt for leading Dash into this mess. Maybe I should have rested first instead of rushing headlong into this.

My reckless side had reappeared, but it was too late now. We weren't getting out without Diana.

That's if we got out at all.

We passed down the next flight with no trouble. It was as if we were being allowed easy access to the hospital. But, as we reached the bottom, the hair on my head stood up, and my skin tingled. I touched Dash's arm and got an electric jolt, making me jump, her fur standing on end.

'You think this has to do with the atomic energy burning outside the building?'

'Either that or it's because of what's inside there.' I pointed to the room ahead.

'The morgue?'

The windows were frosted, so we couldn't see through them, but the pressure at the front of my mind told me something was in there. I touched the door, the charge in the air doing nothing to remove the chill from my palm. I pushed it open, hand and gun pointed forward as we crept into the room, fumbling for the light switch. The smell hit us first, an aroma of something on the edge of death.

Dash coughed up her lungs. 'What the hell is that stink?'

I grabbed my nose. 'I think it's formaldehyde and embalming fluid.'

I found the light switch. The lights flickered on overhead like fireflies preparing for a dance.

'By the Gods,' Dash said as I followed her gaze across the room.

The gloom lifted from our vision, and we stared upon what looked like stacked columns of potato sacks. As I got closer, I understood what was making that terrible odour: bodies were roped together and piled high from the floor to the ceiling. There must have been hundreds.

'Is this how the Japanese used the morgue during the war?'

Dash froze to the spot, but I crept forward, holding my hand over my face in a futile attempt at warding off the smell.

'No, I don't think this is anything to do with the natives of the city.'

The chill grew stronger as I approached the first column of humans, my heart threatening to crack my ribs. The bodies were wrapped in thick cloth, with only their heads exposed. A thin sheet of wood separated each one.

Dash stood by my side. 'Why would the Queens of Heaven keep cadavers like this?'

I wanted to throw up, but I forced myself on. The closest body was a dark-haired woman, eyes closed and head facing the floor. Spectre-like fingers grabbed at my ribs. The woman shivered as her eyelids flickered and opened. Breath escaped from her mouth in short bursts.

I clutched at my throat. 'These people are alive.'

'It's a primitive version of cryogenics. It's the best we could do in this period.' The words came from the shadows. The weapons were ready as we spun around. 'You took your good time getting here.' Her voice was velvet, rubbed against silk. I had the gun pointed at her face as she approached me.

'There's no need for that, Ruby; we're not here to fight you.'

Another woman joined her, long flowing hair like volcanic fire. They could have been twins, one blonde and a redhead, tall and thin as if they hadn't eaten in weeks. I kept the weapon aimed in their direction.

'If you didn't want to hurt us, you should have told your security upstairs.'

The blonde replied. 'They weren't for you. We'll take you to Diana. Follow us.'

They found a gap between the bodies, striding towards the back of the room. We stepped after them. I watched them but couldn't stop glancing at those trussed up on either side of us.

Dash growled behind me. 'Why are these people imprisoned like this?'

We reached the end and another door, the blonde woman turning to us.

'How else would we power the loop?' She pushed the entrance open.

A knot gripped my stomach. So this was where they got the energy for the loop, from living human bodies.

Was Diana responsible for this horror?

The redhead spoke. 'Would you like to see the loop?'

'Aren't we in it?' I said.

'You are, but it needs power to keep it sustained.'

We followed her into a typical hospital ward full of medical equipment and a dozen empty beds. At the far end was something looking like an altar with a font on top. A shimmering sapphire haze surrounded it like a neon aurora. My legs stumbled as I trailed the woman, a sickness growing inside my gut even before I saw the grin on her face. I stared into the middle of the blue vapour and recoiled at the sight: brains sitting like lumps of meat in a bowl of soup.

'Normal brains give off a pitiful amount of energy compared to ours, but if you put enough of them together in the right condition with the appropriate technology, we get a decent battery for our needs. Of course, children's brains are better, so full of imagination and yet to be scarred by the realities of the adult world, but Diana refuses to work with those.'

She peered at the horror in front of me, and I waited for her to scoop up a brain and devour it. I turned away and hung my head, struggling to speak.

Dash put her arm around my waist. 'How do you get out of this loop?'

The two Queens laughed.

'That knowledge is for humans only, furball,' the redhead said.

I bit my tongue. 'Where's Diana?'

'She's waiting for you through there.' The blonde pointed to a door at the side of the room. 'Just you, no pets allowed.'

Dash ignored their hilarity and came to me. 'Don't worry; I'll be fine.'

I brushed her paw and put my fingers on the handle. This was the moment I'd waited for since our reacquaintance on the pier. Now was the time to get all the answers about my missing past.

Chapter 11

The Experiments of Time

It was hard to breathe. I puffed out my chest and forced the door open, greeted by banks of computers.

'You shouldn't be here.' Her voice cut right through me, my legs going weak and my body heading to the ground in a faint. Diana's hand caught me before I hit the floor. 'But it's good to see you.'

She pulled me up and clasped me in her arms. An eternity of barren regrets swirled inside me, alongside a thousand questions. As we drew apart, worry consumed her.

'What are they forcing you to do?' I said.

She guided me towards the computer, her lips close to my head, so only I heard her.

'I have to do more and more of their experiments. But that's not why I'm here.'

She caressed my cheek as a tear slipped down her face.

I fought back my tears. 'Why have they done this?'

Fear gripped her voice as she hung onto my arm. 'They used me as bait to lure you here. You must get away as soon as possible.'

I blurted the words out. 'Is it because you're my granddaughter?'

Diana looked flabbergasted, bursting into laughter loud enough to accompany the destruction outside the loop. She regained her composure. 'Who told you that?'

'Ishtar.'

She shook her head and frowned. 'Don't believe anything she says.'

'Why would they want to lure me here?' I stared at Diana, unsure if I was happy or sad not to be related to her.

'I had information they need, but I cut it out of my head and hid it.' The sadness in her voice matched the sorrow in her expression.

'Like you did with my childhood years?'

I pulled from her, desperate for her to deny it, to claim it was the Watchers or the Queens who'd stolen my memories. Or that they'd forced her to do it.

Her eyes reflected the pain inside me. 'I'm sorry, Ruby, but I had to do it. They wanted what's in your mind. I had to remove everything before you joined us.'

My lips swam in tears. 'Why?'

Diana pushed her head down, her voice like an imminent earthquake.

'I don't know. I also had to keep it from myself, so I

wiped it from my memory. That's why they needed us together, to see what we'd tell each other.'

On cue, the redhead entered the room. 'How is your little reunion coming along?' She grinned. 'I have to say your pet is quite grumpy.'

'You should see her on a bad day.' I pointed the laser pistol at her.

'You think you can shoot your way out of here?' She laughed as she spoke, unable to keep the ridicule from her tone.

I waved the gun in her face. 'Maybe I want to cause you pain as you've done to those poor people stacked in the other room.'

She ignored the threat and pulled a chair next to Diana. 'The only way any of us get out of here is when you two tell us what we want to know.'

'Which is what?' I gripped the pistol even tighter.

She stared at Diana before leering at me. 'Gloriana put something in your head, kid.' Her voice was condescending, her gaze ridiculing me. 'Then Diana took it out, stuck it somewhere and hid it inside someone else. We need that information, or everything will go to crap.'

'You should have thought of that before you ostracised Gloriana from your little cult.'

I held Diana's hand for strength, determined to get everyone out in one piece. The redhead snorted like a clown overdosing on laughing glass.

'Jeez, why does everybody tell me how clever you are when you say such stupid things?' She wiped the smirk from her face. 'Our glorious leader went it alone and disappeared on us, as you did with the Watchers. We'd love to get our hands on her, but we have no idea where or when she is. Do you?'

'Why would I? I want nothing to do with her, the Watchers, or you Queens of Heaven.' I let go of Diana's hand and moved towards the woman who thought she was my captor.

The redhead peered right through me. 'Where are you from, Ruby?'

Before I replied, Dash yelled from the other room, signalling me to raise the gun and whack red in the face. I was getting used to bashing people in the head. She crumpled in a heap. I slipped outside to check on Dash as she stood over the blonde slumped at her feet.

'Time to leave,' she said.

I nodded and returned to Diana. 'How do we get out of here?'

I kept one eye on the woman on the floor. Red moaned and lifted her fingers to the bruise I'd given her. Diana trembled, her eyes downcast and riddled with sadness.

Dash joined us. 'Let's smash that battery of human brains.'

'All that will do is turn off the loop and bring the atomic blast down on all of us.'

Diana knelt near the red-headed woman as she spoke, wiping the blood from her face. There was a connection between the two women I didn't understand.

'So, what's the solution?' I wanted to leave as soon as possible. Diana could answer my questions once we got her to the base.

'We need to generate an energy greater than the atomic blast outside to burst through it and get away,' Diana said.

A low sigh came from the other side of the door as the blonde regained consciousness.

'Can we do that here?' Dash asked Diana.

Diana spoke in rapid bursts. 'One of us needs to

connect to the loop battery and let it syphon off the time energy from our brain. The device will overload, and the subsequent time-displaced explosion will push back the atomic energy and allow the rest of us to jump out of here.'

'Time energy in the brain?' I said.

Was that what Oban had detected in that room on Avon? Was it the same energy that crippled a time traveller when they reappeared near an exit point?

'That's a story for later,' Diana said. 'We have to create a link to the loop battery.'

'I nominate the animal as a sacrifice.' The blonde stood behind Dash with a gun pointed at her neck.

'And you two are coming with us.' The redhead had re-joined the land of the living. 'Ishtar can cut into your brains at her leisure.'

The blonde waved the pistol in Dash's face. 'Move into the other room.'

'You planned this all along?' I said as we headed for the loop generator. Diana looked beaten by the enormity of what was happening.

'We needed the two of you together to find what you stole from us. We hoped you'd bring your pet with you. Otherwise, one of us would have to sacrifice ourselves for the greater cause.'

'And what is this great cause of yours?' I tried to stall for time and think of a way to get the gun away from Dash's head.

'To be young again and live forever,' the redhead replied. 'Only then can we change the course of human history. Now order your pet to stick its paw into the energy field.'

The weapon was too close to Dash's face for me to snatch it away.

Diana moved towards the redhead. 'Let them go, and I'll tell you what you want to know. I'll show you how to use the time energy to restore your youth and immortality.'

Red glanced at her blonde colleague and smiled. 'That's a drink you owe me. I told you she was lying all this time.'

The blonde relaxed and returned the smile. The lapse in concentration was enough for me to lean forward, grab the gun, and fall into her. The movement took us into the wall, the bullet exploding past my ear and burning my skin. As I landed on top of the blonde, Dash shouted something I couldn't understand. An explosion rattled inside my ears as I grappled with the hand holding the pistol. We rolled around on the floor until we hit the base of the energy device, my hip giving it a whack as I struggled with her. I lifted her by the hands before slamming her skull into the concrete beneath us. She went limp under me and dropped the weapon to the side.

'Dash,' I shouted as I climbed off the stricken woman. My head throbbed, and my ears ached from the bells ringing inside them. My vision was blurred, unable to see the others anywhere.

'Over here,' Dash said behind me. I turned, seeing her leaning over Diana and the unconscious redhead. Blood streamed from Diana's stomach, painting a pink canvas on the surrounding ground.

'Diana!' I dropped to my knees and cradled her face. Dash stared at me and shook her head.

Diana's voice shuddered. 'I'm sorry for what I did to you, Ruby.'

Every inch of me froze. 'It doesn't matter now.'

I buried my face in hers, feeling her heart next to mine and knowing she didn't have long left. Two years of memories washed through me as I sobbed in her arms: that first day in the vast library of the Watchers when she talked about travelling through space and time, of the great responsibility she prepared me for, of the bond which grew between us in that time; of the love I came to have for her. All my doubts about her dissipated as life slipped from her.

'I have one last thing to tell you.' She pulled away from me. 'But take me to the generator first.'

Tears prickled at my eyes as she had one final sacrifice to give. But, as I lifted her, all the secrets and lies were inconsequential; I knew whatever she'd done had been for my benefit.

'I've got her,' Dash said as she helped me get Diana to the loop generator.

Hanging onto my friend, I stared into the sapphire glow containing the dreadful sight of those vibrating brains, a lump in my stomach reminding me of the horrors I still had to face.

'When I put my hand into it, there will be a connection to the time energy inside me,' Diana said as the darkness increased around her eyes. 'It will suck the power out of me, causing a release to push back the atomic energy surrounding us. You'll know it's happening because this blue aurora will shimmer into yellow: that's when you need to trigger your leaving.'

As she spoke, Diana collapsed in my arms. My face was soaked with tears as I thrust my head into hers.

'Goodbye, Diana,' I whispered into her ear. She pushed her lips close to me.

'Look for Gretel and her breadcrumbs. That's where you'll find what they stole from you.' She moved from me and plunged her arm into the blue light. Sparks flashed from the intrusion point.

Dash pulled me backwards. 'When it turns yellow, we leave.'

I wiped my cheeks. The two Watchers were awake and pushed their bodies up from the floor.

'Noooo!' the redhead screamed.

'Let's go home,' I said to Dash as the air changed colour, and I watched the life drain from Diana.

We left as the sound of thunder descended upon the building.

Chapter 12

Blitz Kids

Diana's face had haunted me for as long as I could remember, but now the vision in my head had changed; it wasn't the smile she'd given me as I'd escaped from the Watchers, but that last expression of pain as she thrust her arm into the time loop generator.

Everything was a blur when we reappeared at the base.

'Ruby,' Dash said as I pushed past her and went to my room. I locked the door behind me, and she didn't enter. I heard her speaking to Daisy and Lucy, but my mind was somewhere else; somewhere I didn't want it to be.

I stood near the bed, my legs unmoving, as numb as the rest of me. A great weight pressed down on my shoulders and I couldn't move. There were no mirrors in my room, but I had a sudden urge to peer into my face to see if I'd changed on the outside. Inside me, all was different, whereas before, I'd cultivated my isolation into a strength. Now it cut into my heart and shredded it.

What did I look like now? Did I still appear to be somebody without a care in the world, even though I was changing history and altering lives? Was there a glimpse in my eyes of someone seeking danger and revelling in risks, of only feeling alive when facing death?

My eyelids grew heavy, transmitting a signal of despair through my veins that infected every sinew and bone, turning my blood into liquid metal. I sank onto the bed and rolled into the middle. The strength that it took left me drained.

Then I drifted in and out of sleep. I had two years of memories of Diana locked inside my head, but I didn't reach for them, knowing they would make me feel worse.

After a while, I got up, my despair transforming into rage. I touched my cheeks and nearly burnt my fingers. The strength returned to my legs as I stomped across the room and swept my hand over the shelf, sending books and ornaments crashing to the floor. A vintage Mickey Mouse figurine cracked its head on a table leg while my favourite Valkyrie bobbled-headed doll bounced off the carpet and rolled into a copy of *Do Androids Dream of Electric Sheep*. I grabbed a CD of *Screamadelica* and threw it at the wall. The case shattered on impact and vomited its contents everywhere.

'Are you okay, Ruby?' Dash said from the other side of the door.

I took a deep breath and opened it. 'Nothing a stiff drink won't fix.'

She gazed into my eyes before pouring me a large whiskey with ice. My emotions were in turmoil, and I didn't want to expose Daisy or her mother to that. Dash gave me the booze, and I let it warm my throat, hoping it would do the same with my heart.

But it didn't.

Dash poured a glass for herself. 'How do you feel, Ruby?'

I pushed an ice cube into my cheek and sat on the bed. 'We need to change what happened in Nagasaki.'

She narrowed her. 'What, prevent Diana's death?'

I bit through the ice, and its edge cut into my lip. My blood was warm, but even that couldn't remove the chill running through my veins.

'Yes, Dash; that's what we do – we stop people from dying. I changed centuries of Kaladanian history, so why not this as well?'

She sat next to me. 'You're grieving, Ruby; I get that, but you can't keep playing God with the past.'

I jerked up and snapped at her. 'How can you understand, Dash? I lost my best friend.'

As soon as I spoke, I knew it was a mistake. She could have chastised me, reminding me of her planet's destruction and the death of all her people. And pointed out how much of a friend she was to me.

She finished her drink and stood. 'You must grieve, Ruby. I've explained everything to Lucy and Daisy. I'll be outside if you need anything.'

Dash touched my hand as she left. I put my glass on the side and lay on the bed, closing my eyes and hoping for sleep. But it took a long time coming, only after I'd spent an age repeating my last moments with Diana. I stayed alone for twenty-four hours in my room, engulfed by the darkness inside and out. When I stepped back into the light, I discovered Dash and Lucy discussing Daisy's future. The kid was conspicuous by her absence.

Lucy hugged me. 'I'm sorry for your loss, Ruby.'

I thanked her, desperate to talk about anything else. 'Is Daisy okay?'

Lucy sighed. 'I've tried to catch Daisy up with her studies, but I'm no teacher, and she never liked school.' She sounded downhearted. 'It didn't matter which one she went to or what the teachers promised; the other kids always picked on her.'

Dash reached out and put her paw across Lucy's hand. 'Was it because she was cleverer than them?'

Lucy nodded. 'None of the older children liked her because she was much younger and brighter than them. I was at my wit's end before....'

'So, what's the solution?' I spoke before Lucy could remind us all of her passing. We'd all had enough of death.

'The whole of space and time is our educational oyster,' Dash said.

Dash smiled at me, but she couldn't hide the worry from her eyes. She'd told me to grieve for Diana, but I wasn't sure I knew how. We'd been apart for a long time, with my recent thoughts consumed by doubts over what she'd done to me. I'd suffered through the sadness and the anger, but now I didn't know what I felt.

I watched Daisy and her mother joking around, teasing Dash about her extravagant Victorian clothing. It was joyous to see them like that, and the irony wasn't lost on me that I was the watcher in the room. My motivation was to avenge Diana. The Queens and the Watchers were two sides of the same coin as far as I was concerned, but leaving them alone was out of the question.

The Time Ring had left a slight mark on my finger, a shadow to show me what I once was because I was different now the technology was grafted to my spine. Sometimes, I thought I felt it moving inside me, but I put that down to my brain playing tricks on me. It had given me a new power, that ability to take living things with me to any point in space and time. What had happened on Kaladan with the Yoron was only the start. Nothing was beyond me now. Still, I knew I had to stop rushing into things. People close to me needed my protection. So I focused on Daisy's future.

'What schooling would you like for your daughter, Lucy?'

Before she could answer, Daisy ran into the room. 'I want a robot teacher.'

I was unsurprised to see her lips covered in chocolate. One of us would need to have a serious word with her about diet.

'Human or otherwise, the first task is to get someone – or thing – to teach you about nutrition and healthy eating.'

I grabbed for her, but she dodged my reach and scampered to the computers.

'I read about the teaching bots from the twenty-second century.' She pointed cream-drenched fingers at the screen. 'I'll have one of them.'

Dash slid over. 'We could combine it with a security droid to monitor her when we're not here.'

It sounded like an excellent idea. I moved towards the screens, and Daisy must have thought I was trying to catch her again. She sprang up like a jack-in-the-box and ran around the room, pretending to be some futuristic flying machine. She was full of boundless energy; maybe it was something to do with all the sugar she consumed.

'I want to learn everything, Ruby, like how Diana taught you about history, space, time, and everything in the universe.'

Her effervescence counteracted the darkness that threatened to drag me into the abyss at the mention of Diana's name.

'Would you like to go back to school?' I said.

Daisy sat next to me in front of the computers. 'You and Dash can teach me – and maybe one of those robot teachers.'

Her eyes sparkled like the stars. 'What about being with other kids your age and making friends? It can't all be about spending time with adults.'

She crossed her arms and looked older than her mother. 'Kids are silly. They mess around all the time.'

I didn't know what to say since I had no recollections of my childhood, not knowing if it was enjoyable.

Lucy Lynx rescued me from a tricky situation. 'Dash told me you came back from Nagasaki with a clue to your stolen past.'

Stolen past? Yes, that's precisely what it was, even if Diana had said she'd removed my memories to stop the Queens of Heaven from using them for some unknown purpose. Unknown, but guaranteed not to be good for anybody but themselves.

'Diana told me to look for Gretel and her breadcrumbs. That's where I'll find what they stole from me.'

'They?' Lucy said.

'I think she meant the Queens of Heaven.'

Lucy nodded. 'And they're the splinter group from the

Watchers? The ones who want to change history and not only observe and record it?'

Dash rubbed at her chin. 'But that makes little sense, Ruby. Diana said she removed knowledge from your memories – and hers – so the Queens couldn't access it. So if anybody stole from you, it was Diana.'

Daisy puffed out her cheeks. 'Diana nicked it from you to stop the Queens from having it. And she wiped bits from her brain to stop them from getting that. Is that right?'

I nodded as I looked at Dash, aware that neither of us had wanted to address that after Diana's sacrifice. I glanced at the information on the computer screen.

'Were you busy while I rested?'

'I had to do something,' Dash said.

'You searched through all the references for Hansel and Gretel?'

'Well, I got the computers to find them. There are over six million hits.' Dash sounded as disappointed as I was.

'That's worse than a needle in a haystack. Why couldn't Diana have told me straight out what she meant?'

Grief and frustration coursed through me like a toxic cocktail. And I guessed why she'd been so enigmatic with her words: she was complicit in what was done to me, and the guilt must have crippled her.

As I spoke, Daisy jumped from the chair, running to the other end of the room. She returned and dropped a magazine in my lap.

'Spies,' she said. 'They were snooping on her, so she had to speak in code.'

'What?' I said.

The kid beamed at me. 'You have to crack the puzzle, Ruby. Diana couldn't tell you the truth because those horrible Queens were spying on her. So what she told you was in code.' She shone her smile on all of us. 'So now we have to work together like an Enigma machine.'

I stared at her and realised why she'd got bored at every school Lucy had sent her to. Then I grabbed the mag and gazed at the photo of Daniel Craig as James Bond on the cover.

'Daisy's right. The Queens of Heaven were expecting us to go there to rescue Diana – and they wanted to see what she said to me. So they would have bugged the place.'

The kid grinned as she snatched the magazine from me. Dash pointed at the screen.

'Gretel and her breadcrumbs were not much to go on. But I got three results when I did an advanced search for that combination of words.'

I scrutinised them. The first two were posts on a blog from 2010, someone waxing lyrical about their love for peppers, using the term as a simile. The third was a Reddit post for house cleaning.

I scrunched up my fist and slammed it on the desk. 'What have peppers and house cleaning got to do with Diana's experiments and my missing memories?'

My internal fury abated as I tried not to upset our guests, but they ignored me anyway. Daisy scampered around the room, pretending she was a plane about to crash, diving towards Lucy sitting cross-legged on the floor. Lucy caught the kid full-on, and they fell backwards, tumbling into a pile of dusty 1980s pop music magazines. Mother and daughter laughed as they crumpled into each other, surrounded by shiny bits of paper.

I gave up staring at the data on the screen and turned to the Lynx girls fooling around amongst the photos of '80s pop stars. Daisy dug her fingers into some shiny paper, squeezed it in her hand, and brought it up to her face.

'Gretel and the Breadcrumbs, here they are.'

I nearly fell out of the chair. 'What?'

She held the magazine in the air. 'Here's a review of a concert they played.'

I stumbled out of the seat, knees hitting the floor and sliding towards the kid. I snatched the paper from her fingers and scrutinised the small text box near the back of the magazine. Dash peered over my shoulder as I read it aloud.

'Gretel and the Breadcrumbs deliver the sound of the zeitgeist through the purest electronic waves. They make fine additions to the Blitz Kid movement.'

That was it, two sentences. And the date of the gig was May 2, 1980. I handed the magazine to Dash, who took it to the computer and entered the details into the search engine.

'No results for this but a quarter of a million for Blitz Kids.'

'My mother was a Blitz Kid,' Lucy said.

'Your mother was in the Blitz?' I said.

'No, silly; it was a club in Covent Garden in the early eighties where people went to dress up and listen to music.'

Daisy pulled a face and squeezed her chin. 'Oh, Mum.'

I flipped the magazine to the front and stared at a glossy photograph of Kate Bush, looking moody.

'Blitz and blitz.' The words swirled around inside my head and out of my mouth.

Dash turned away from the computer. 'What are you thinking?'

I touched the cover, the faded gloss bristling against my skin. How long had those magazines sat in that pile? It had to be over twenty years, at least.

'We rescued Ursula from the Blitz in 1940. Then Daisy discovers that Gretel and the Breadcrumbs played a club called the Blitz in 1980, information inside a magazine which has been here for over two decades.'

Lucy picked up the rest of the magazines. Numerous outrageously dressed men and women stared out from the covers, idols from when sparkly brightness infected the country's mood. I puckered my lips and formulated a hasty plan.

'I guess you're off to 1980s London.'

I grabbed her paws. 'Not without you, Dash.'

'You don't think my appearance will scare people?'

'Tish and posh, my friend; you'll fit right in with the new romantics with that natural fur. Now let's sort out some appropriate clothes for our trip.'

My recklessness had returned, and I felt good.

Chapter 13

Ruby's Diary

Day Eight Hundred and One, Year Three

E arth Time: 2232. Location: Kostuk. (Planet Pegula).

The medical centre was in the poorest part of town, a million miles from the facilities few could afford. We took the bus there, Charles rushing to sit upstairs as if he was a young boy again. Elizabeth hoped he wouldn't have an incident. To display any instability in public would be an immediate black mark on both their records. If she couldn't keep him under control, there was the risk of being placed in custody, where appropriate help would be non-existent. The State called them National Care Centres, but they were little more than prisons for those with mental health issues.

'I'll never let Charles end up in one of those,' Elizabeth said as we got our seats near him at the back of the bus. She squeezed my hands. 'I don't know how to thank you for this.'

Her smile warmed my heart, but I knew it would be unlikely to get better for them. He placed a hand on the glass and gazed out the window, peering at the landscape as it changed from busy shops and new flats to run-down industrial areas and dilapidated housing estates. I thought about where I'd spent most of the last two years, inside that library with Diana, living an isolated life far from the realities of the universe. She'd drummed it into me about never changing history, but I'd known I could never stand by and watch people suffer when I could do something about it. Being on Pegula had only cemented my conviction, and staring at Elizabeth and Charles increased my desire to help them.

But what could I do?

The bus arrived at our stop, and Elizabeth led him off. I followed and stepped into an aroma of dead animals and human waste. The streets were narrow and poorly lit, with tall buildings looming on either side. The pavement was cracked and uneven, littered with trash and debris. The houses were dilapidated, their windows boarded up or broken. Graffiti covered the walls, and shouting and arguing erupted behind closed doors.

We dodged the wild dogs sniffing around the rubbish strewn across the street. I ignored the whispers slipping from the shadowed corners leading to the health centre. The ground floor had been converted into small units housing beds for the homeless, while the makeshift medical centre was upstairs underneath stained glass windows. I led them up and into the heart of the former church to a doctor I'd spoken to yesterday. It had cost me two days' wages, but the money meant nothing to me. And the visit was the world to them.

I left them with the doctor and slipped into another room. Looking tired and worn, people of all ages filled the small, cramped space. The air was thick with the scent of antiseptic and sweat. The only light came from a single fluorescent bulb overhead, casting a pale glow over everything. I peered at their faces in the flickering illumination, seeing haunted, desperate expressions.

In one corner, a young mother sat with a baby on her lap, both looking feverish and ill. The baby's cries echoed off the walls, adding to the general misery. Opposite them was an older man hunched over, his breathing laboured and ragged. He clutched a cloth bag tightly to his chest as if it held all his worldly possessions.

The rest of the people sat on wooden benches, their eyes fixed on the door that led to the examination rooms. They waited patiently, some with their heads in their hands, others staring blankly into space. I turned from them, went to the window, and gazed into the street outside.

I saw a group of children playing in an alleyway, their laughter and shouts a stark contrast to the ominous atmosphere everywhere else. I couldn't help but feel a twinge of sadness as I realised this was their reality, growing up in such a dangerous and impoverished environment. Then I noticed their smiles, knowing they had something to enjoy in their young, difficult lives. I watched them in the street and pictured a younger version of me joining their games, seeing a smile on that other me and feeling the pain in my heart. Then I pushed it aside as Elizabeth and

Charles left the doctor's office. She nodded to me and showed me the folder in her hand.

'I've got the scans.'

Charles shuffled next to her as they went downstairs and out of the building. I caught up with her.

'How was it?'

He peered at his feet as she revealed the results. 'The doctor said it's frontotemporal dementia. There are black holes behind Charles's eyes and close to the ears, where the cells have shrunk and died. And they're getting bigger.'

I watched as she fought back the tears, realising there was no cure. Even with all my travels through time and space, I understood that nothing could help him.

Charles peered over her shoulder. 'I like those photographs. They resemble giant avocados with dark canals crisscrossing them.'

Elizabeth smiled at him and spoke to Ruby. 'He was a keen amateur avant-garde photographer when we first met. He took photos of fashion models covered in tiny plastic eyes, and a row of monkeys descending in size, sitting on a horse, and one time he asked me to wear a dress made from real flowers.' She gazed wistfully at him. 'But those were the days when art, like science, wasn't frowned upon, and creativity wasn't dangerous to the social order.'

I didn't know what to say as we waited for the bus. On the way back, she clutched the scans to her chest as if she could absorb what was on them, and it would cure the blackness infecting his brain.

Elizabeth thanked me again when we returned to the flats. 'You should come for dinner tomorrow night.' I agreed and said I'd be there for seven. 'Are you old enough to drink?'

I laughed. 'I'll brink a bottle of red and a bottle of

white.'

'Bring cider for me,' Charles said as I went inside.

So that's what I did.

Of course, the alcohol was only the equivalent of Earth booze, but my translator converted the terms into something I understood in English.

'How was work?' Elizabeth said as I handed over the drink.

'I'm not sure I'll be there much longer,' I said as I sat opposite the bit TV. She took the bottles to the kitchen and spoke to me from there.

'How come?'

There was a noise from upstairs, and I assumed it was Charles.

'I need something more stimulating.' I'd taken the job for the monotony, but after discovering Elizabeth and Charles's problems, had realised I was wasting my time in that office when it could be better spent helping people.

She returned with two glasses. 'I hope that doesn't mean you're leaving the neighbourhood?'

I sipped the wine, and it chilled the back of my throat. 'Well, I won't be here forever.' I changed the subject. 'Something smells wonderful in the kitchen.'

'It's my favourite, roast chicken smoked in a barbecue sauce,' Charles said as he came downstairs. He'd shaved and combed his hair, knocking ten years off his appearance.

Elizabeth handed him a glass of cider. 'To new friends and good neighbours.'

'Thank you for the drink,' he said as he went to the kitchen.

She sidled up to me. 'This is one of his better days.' She

drank half of her wine. 'This is when I think nothing has changed in our lives and everything is perfect again.'

'The food is ready,' he announced.

'Go, sit,' Elizabeth said as she went to help him.

It was the first civilised meal I'd ever had with anybody apart from Diana. And it was great. Charles was quiet, having slipped into his looking lost state. Occasionally, the taste of the meal would bring him out of it, and he'd gaze at his wife. Then, when we finished, he took her hand in his.

'Sometimes, it all comes back to me, and I remember who I was.' He beamed at her. 'And I know I've loved you forever.'

When his grin dissipated, Elizabeth broke into a tsunami of tears, and he resumed staring at the wall. I washed up when she took him to bed. Then, when she returned, she refreshed our glasses.

She raised hers to me. 'An eternity of pain is worthwhile for those fleeting moments of hope and joy.'

'What will you do now?' I said.

Elizabeth dragged her legs underneath her on the sofa. 'All I can do, Ruby, is take each day as it comes.' She sipped at her drink. 'But enough about me. Tell me about you and how you ended up here.'

It pained me to lie to her, but I had no choice. 'My parents died when I was young, and an aunt raised me. I left her a few months ago, and here I am.' It was the same story I'd used to create my fake records.

'You poor thing,' she said.

We finished the wine and spent the rest of the night discussing everything but our families. It felt like my first grown-up conversation, yet Diana was never far from my thoughts. When I returned to my flat and went to bed, I wondered how I would leave this place, knowing I had to.

Chapter 14

The Music of Time

Dash played with Daisy as I went through our clothes in the basement, looking for something suitable for the Blitz Club. I searched my memories for the last time I'd visited England in the 1980s. It was the summer of '89, long before I met Dash, and I spent a night dancing and handing out smiley face badges. I was sure I still had a stack of those somewhere. And a pair of baggy jeans.

'Oh, wow,' Lucy said as she joined me. 'You've got some great stuff here.'

I smiled. 'One of the benefits of time travel.'

She flicked through a rack of dresses stretching from Victorian straight jackets disguised as corsets to the shortest of short outfits.

'Imagine what would happen if you wore the wrong outfit for the wrong time.' She grabbed a mini-skirt. 'This wouldn't have amused Queen Victoria at all.'

I laughed. 'I don't know. Vicki was impressed when she met Dash.'

Lucy put a hand to her face. 'What?'

'Yes, it was 1832, and the future Queen was twelve or thirteen, still known as Alexandrina Victoria. She thought she was dreaming, but she loved Dash.' I smiled at the memory. 'It was our relationship's early days, and Dash assumed we could take little Vicki with us. I don't think she's ever forgiven me for that.'

Lucy put the mini-skirt back on the rack and touched my arm.

'I never knew my father, so my mother brought me up alone. She died when Daisy was young, which was probably a good thing. My mother was already three-quarters gone before she passed. Dementia stripped her of almost everything I recognised from the woman who raised me and who I once adored. It's terrible to say, but when at last what was left of her died, I felt an immense relief, for she and we suffered so much, and the mother I loved left me long before the end came. I turned my grief into sadness and then into a memory.'

'I'm sorry, Lucy,' I said.

She nodded. 'You'll grieve in your own time and in your own way.' She glanced behind her to where Daisy was scrambling over Dash's head. 'I don't know whether to talk to her about my death or not. I guess not since I'm here with her now.' She smiled at me. 'Some people will experience

109

profound sadness and apathy when grieving; others won't. Some might find that sadness hits them one day like a dart in the heart as they stand in line at the supermarket. The variability of human emotion and resilience is infinite. The only guarantee for all of us is that time will pass and, as it does, we will inevitably adapt to loss. That's what our brains do: adapt. You'll suffer, Ruby, but you'll survive. And all of us are here for you.'

I dragged her to me and hugged her. 'Thank you.'

'Are we ready?' Dash said from the other room.

I let go of Lucy as Daisy barged into her mother.

'Show me what you're wearing!' the kid shouted.

So I did.

Twenty minutes later, we stood squashed inside a group of outlandishly attired people. Dash had gone for a one-piece science-fiction-inspired grey suit, where a slim white stripe made a diagonal cut from her shoulder to her waist on the other side. Pointed black ankle boots finished her combination. Her furry face grinned at everyone who stared at her. I'd settled on a down-at-heel private eye from a film noir look, complete with a suit, hat and tie.

Daylight had vanished as we got there, and the night was another country. Yet, inside the club, lives sparkled and blossomed in ways they couldn't outside in the grim and gloom of 1980s Britain. On the other side of the walls was darkness begging for energy, while all life was present in the Blitz. A heady air of alcohol and anticipation fought through the strains of Roxy and Kraftwerk as the music faded into nothingness, and trembling desire floated through the crowd.

A bloke resembling a stuffed peacock skipped onto the

stage. His ebony-lined eyes were subdued and sunken, with rainbow-splashed hair exploding from his head as if a rocket had gone off in a fireworks shop. He had a glass of bourbon in one hand and a bottle of beer in the other, as if unable to decide which to drink first. Then he announced the band.

'Ladies and gentlemen, boys and girls, pirates and pompadours, I give you Gretel and the Breadcrumbs.'

Nobody in the crowd moved or spoke. I was in the middle, Dash near the stage. She'd already gathered a small group of admirers around her, gazing at a costume that good, exclaiming how fabulous her makeup was, wondering if she was in the next *Star Wars* movie. The band arrived at an ocean of dry ice that seeped up from the floor and swirled across the throng like mist descending from the Andes. It chilled my bones as I stared at them. They were dressed in pristine white suits, wearing the most lifelike Marlene Dietrich masks I'd ever seen. The audience continued their best impersonation of frozen statues. I was unsure what to expect, ready for anything and everything. Diana's clue had sent us to the club, but I didn't know what we were looking for.

A low hum slipped from the keyboards flanking the singer, joining the manufactured smoke drifting from the floor, swirling up through our bones and nestling in the back of my neck. So it was only electronic music at its minimalist inception until she sang: a voice crafted somewhere between Nina Simone and Polly Jean Harvey. It was everything the electronica wasn't – warm, soulful and brimming with the mysteries of life. They were the perfect combination, good enough to stimulate the people surrounding me.

The crowd swayed as the music vibrated through the floor and into the rafters. I scanned the room for anything unusual, finding that everything was. Like every gig I'd ever been to, and that's a lot, I ended up next to the punters yapping the loudest.

'I didn't come here to watch this shit,' a slurred male voice behind me said.

'So why are you here?' was the sober reply.

'I'm waiting for the celeb to arrive,' the drunk said as I contemplated turning to punch him in the face.

'Which celeb would that be?'

'Bowie,' was the reply.

'That's umpossible,' a third voice said. I spun on hearing that word, staring at my impossibility.

'Gideon,' I said.

His fingers caressed the extravagant Elizabethan rough around his neck as he grinned at me. I lunged at him, only to be pushed aside by the shoulder of somebody looking like Boy George.

'Do you really want to hurt him?' George said as Gideon disappeared into the horde.

Gideon's presence could only mean one thing. I moved to look for Dash. The music increased as the crowd encircled me like a human blanket. There were men dressed as unemployed clowns and Victorian dandies, while the women were a mixture of femme fatale flappers, chic glamour pusses, and futuristic ingénues. They were more interested in looking at each other than the band. A group near the stage appeared mesmerised by Dash, gabbing away while she sipped her champagne. She waved at me, her face glistening like a supernova.

'You'll never believe it, Ruby, but one of these wonderful peacocks told me they're expecting David Bowie here tonight.'

She'd forgotten our mission, her eyes glittering with the thought of meeting her hero.

Before I could reply, a group of women looking like Lauren Bacall in *The Big Sleep* bundled into me, knocking me sideways and into the wall. My shoulder cracked against the concrete, and a shiver of electricity ran through me. By the time I recovered, several dandy highwaymen were occupying the space between Dash and me.

I slammed past a bloke dressed like Dick Turpin and sidled up to Dash.

'Gideon is here.'

Her smile vanished instantly, handing the drink to one of her new devotees and following me in the direction I'd lost Gideon.

Dash scanned the crowd before turning back to me. 'Gloriana must be with him.'

She pushed by the people at my side. The music went through a quiet phase, the synths squeaking to the low warble of the singer's voice, rising to a crescendo as she hit the height of her powers.

It's a truth never known that Vampires live on the moon
Flying there and back, shaped as succulent bats
Vampires on the moon
Vampires on the moon
They never suck or bite
Unless you say it's all right
Vampires on the moon
Vampires on the moon

The lyrics amused me as I searched for Gideon. I thought I glimpsed him, heading away from the multitude towards a seated area in the corner. I stepped past the huddled groups ahead of me. Another surprise greeted me as I reached the side: Gloriana sat between two women dressed as pirates.

'Are you stalking me?' I said to her.

She pouted and whispered to the pirate on her left before turning to me.

'Ruby, I'd like to introduce you to my friends, Anne Bonny and Mary Read.'

I recognised the names. Fearsome red curls dropped from underneath Anne Bonny's hat as she raised her glass of sparkling green liquid. Inside her tight-fitting leather jacket was the glint of a cutlass and a gun far too sophisticated for this age.

'Gran' 'ealth ter yer lassie.'

She had a musical lilt to her Irish brogue, and I didn't need the translator to break through her accent. I tipped my imaginary fedora to her.

Mary Read wore an eighteenth-century Royal Navy captain's uniform, including long white socks, cravat and tricorn hat. She scowled at me through chestnut eyes before leaning over to kiss Bonny on the lips. I waited a minute for them to separate and addressed Gloriana.

'Are they here for your protection?'

'Yes,' she replied, 'but not from you.'

She nodded at something behind me. I turned to see Ishtar and two of her Queens of Heaven striding towards us. They sparkled in the neon light shimmering above us, looking resplendent in their purple jackets and flared trousers as if they'd stepped off a futuristic aeroplane.

I smiled at them. 'It's nice that you dressed appropriately for the occasion.'

'Step away from the renegade,' Ishtar said.

I didn't know if she was talking about Gloriana or me.

I stood my ground. 'Who's following whom here?'

Ishtar pointed at Gloriana. 'Whatever she told you, it was a lie.'

The pirates bristled, reaching for the weapons inside their clothes. I didn't argue with the statement.

I turned my back on Gloriana and faced Ishtar. 'Diana is not my granddaughter. You lied to me.'

She shrugged. 'How naïve of you, Ruby. Duplicity is the driving force behind everything. You even lie to yourself.'

I'd had enough of her witchery of fiction, determined to leave these Watchers to deal with their squabbles. Then Dash was by my side as Gideon and two men joined Gloriana and her pirates.

'She's all yours,' I said to Ishtar as I took Dash's arm and dragged us into the crowd. The music was at its height as some punters gave up posing for their contemporaries and bounced around the dance floor. Dash grabbed my waist, and we span our way to the stage, bumping elbows with highwaymen and gigolos, courtesans and debutantes.

'What will we do about those?' She nodded toward Gloriana and the others.

The music increased as the singer approached the end of the song.

Pandora's vanished on the highway
Searching for Hope across all of space and time
But all is gone, all is gone
All is gone
All is gone
When many lives become one

I moved closer to Dash to make myself heard.

'They can tear themselves apart for all I care. I want to know why Diana led us here. I need to understand why my past is missing.'

We forced our way to the edge of the stage, looking up as Gretel completed her song.

> *But all is gone, all is gone*
> *When many lives become one*
> *When many lives become one*

As the synths came crashing together, the unmistakable sound of a laser pistol assaulted my ears. The aroma of acrid burning drifted across the club as I twisted my head to see people pushed to the ground as Gideon grappled with Ishtar. Mary and Anne scuffled with the Queens. Most of the audience ignored the fisticuffs in their midst, concentrating on the band as they finished their set.

A surge behind us took me away from Dash and forced me to bend over the front of the stage, my face close to the singer's rose-coloured shoes. The ringing in my ears was a combination of the crowd, the group and the screaming coming from the corner where several time travellers were fighting over something I wanted no part of. I lost sight of Dash, and my shoulder cut into a speaker as somebody tapped my head.

'Come with us,' she said through the Dietrich mask, holding a hand down to me as the fragrance of burning flesh blew around the venue. I reached for those fingers as she lifted me with ease and pulled me towards the back of the stage, hoping Dash had seen what was happening.

The band member dragged me through an exit into a narrow corridor, never looking back at the confusion in the club. Electric lights flickered on the walls as I ran my free hand over the cracked paint and fresh graffiti. The place stank of vomit and urine as we stumbled around two corners and then into another room. Then she let go of me and slammed the door behind us, flicking the lock across.

As my dizzy head and dazed vision adjusted to the new environment, I saw the rest of the band at the back. Empty beer bottles and bits of half-eaten food littered the floor. The noise from the bar had transferred into the four chambers of my heart, creating spasms of excitement surging through me. A rat scurried out of view as I coughed a violent expulsion of phlegm across a tatty-looking sofa. It was the cue for Gretel and the Breadcrumbs to unmask.

'Welcome to 1980, Fourteen.' My rescuer held out her hand. 'I'm Eighteen, and these are Sixteen and Seventeen.'

The other two stepped forward as my hands shook and my jaw hit the floor.

I stared at three versions of myself.

Chapter 15

The Ripples of Time

They looked a little older, but they were me.

Gretel and the Breadcrumbs were me.

The room spun around me, and I thought I was hallucinating again. Dizziness washed over me, and my body trembled. A fog settled over my eyes, and I grabbed a table to steady my legs. It was wet with spilt beer; sticking my fingers together as I pulled them away from the discarded food and cigarette ash. I sucked in stale air and took a deep breath, but it only made me want to throw up.

I slumped into a chair, and something damp seeped into

my trousers. A firestorm swept through my brain as I put my head between my knees, trying to steady my breathing. The nausea was subsiding, but the dizziness was still there. I could hear Donna Summer warbling about feeling love somewhere in the distance. I rubbed my eyes and felt the scar on my skull. Maybe Dr Zante hadn't removed the communication device from my brain, and Ishtar was messing with my mind again. Or perhaps this was a side effect of the Yoron peering into my mind.

'I guess Diana didn't tell you about us,' Eighteen said.

'Fragments,' was all my stuttering lips could say.

Eighteen grabbed a beer and offered it to me. 'Drink?'

I closed my eyes. When I reopened them, the other versions of me were still there.

'What is this? Who are you?'

Eighteen spoke again. 'You know who we are, Fourteen; at least you used to. We are you, and you are us.'

Vertigo crashed through my skull, a cacophony of sounds mixing with the noise from the main room. I sucked in a large gulp of air and let it out slowly.

'Do you remember the first fourteen years of your life?' I said to all of them. They shook their heads in unison.

'Diana didn't have time to train or prepare us; we didn't get any Time Rings.' Eighteen showed me her bare fingers. 'She left us here and said to wait for you.'

My body gave way as she spoke, slumping into the dirty chair and snatching the booze from her. I gulped from it, letting the gaseous liquid warm the insides of my throat.

I wanted to throw up. But I didn't, glancing between them and not liking what I saw.

'Tell me what you know about Diana.'

The younger girls looked at Eighteen as if she was their leader.

'Not a lot, Fourteen. She saved us from something terrible; we all appreciate that.' Fifteen and Sixteen nodded together. 'And she said we had to hide here and wait for you.'

I'd gone looking for my past and discovered three fragments of futures I never had. So why had Diana done this? I finished the beer and dropped the bottle to the floor, where it shattered. I peered down into my broken reflections, watching them move without me stirring my head.

'What's the plan?' Eighteen said as I raised my eyes to see her standing over me.

Sixteen and Seventeen held hands and looked pensive.

'Was there a Fifteen?' I asked them.

'We don't know what happened to her,' Sixteen and Seventeen said in stereo.

Were there any others?

I gazed at them. 'Do you know why Diana plucked you out of time?' All three shook their heads as one. 'And you can't hop through time and space?'

'No,' they said together.

Eighteen stared at me. 'Diana dropped us here a year ago. She gave us money and said to start a band. So tonight was our first proper gig.'

My heart sank into my chest as I plunged into the chair. I gazed at these versions of myself, who knew as little as I did about Diana's plan.

'You've been here twelve months?'

Eighteen grinned at me. 'It's been cool. We had plenty of money, somewhere to stay, and the equipment to play music. What more could a teenage girl want?'

Seventeen kicked the broken glass away from my feet. Then she ran her fingers through her extravagant peacock hairstyle.

'Steve Strange showed me how to do my hair, and Boy George helped with our makeup.'

Considering what was happening outside this room, they seemed pretty upbeat.

'But you knew you'd been brought here through time and into the past?' I said.

'Of course,' Eighteen said. 'Diana promised it was to keep us safe from the Queens of Heaven, but she never explained why.'

Sixteen stepped forward, and I stared into a living mirror, wondering how any of this was possible.

Fragments.

She reached into her jacket and removed a paperback. 'We all read a lot for inspiration and lyrics, and I've looked for as many time travel books as possible. This is my favourite.'

She showed me the cover of Octavia E. Butler's *Kindred*.

Four minutes may have elapsed since we'd entered the room, but it felt like an eternity. I struggled to come to terms with what was happening as I remembered I'd left Dash outside with the warring Watchers and Queens of Heaven. I had to return to her, but I couldn't leave these versions of myself behind.

And then a strange thought struck me.

What if these three weren't fragments of me snatched from different timelines, but they were something else?

What if they were clones?'

The technology for human cloning wouldn't exist on Earth for another century, but it was possible in other parts of the universe.

But if they were clones, who created them and why?

I scrutinised all three again. 'How much time did each of you spend with Diana?'

They glanced at each other before Eighteen spoke. 'Not long, a couple of months before she brought us here.'

'And I was with you?'

They answered together. 'Yes.'

'And Fifteen too?'

Sixteen and Seventeen lowered their heads, but I saw the tears in their eyes as Eighteen replied.

'She was, for a time.'

More questions were forming in my brain when I heard a familiar voice.

'Are you in there, Ruby?'

Dash banged on the door. Eighteen nodded to Seventeen, and they let my friend in.

Her eyes found mine before she realised who else was with us. 'This can't be happening.'

I grabbed another bottle from the table. 'Tell me about it. What happened upstairs?'

Before Dash could reply, gunfire rattled into the door, and the handle shattered into a dozen pieces. A smiling Gideon pushed through the debris as swirling and acrid smoke clung to his frame. I gripped my seat as he pointed his weapon at Eighteen.

He grinned at me, his teeth sparkling through crooked lips. 'If you disappear, I shoot these three and the cat.'

I ignored his threat. 'What's happening with your boss and the others?'

I could hop near to Gideon and take him away before he could fire, but it would weaken me when I returned to this time. And I couldn't abandon these versions of me, not now. I'd gone looking for my past and found three futures I never knew existed.

But Dash could leave.

I glared at her, telling her to take off without saying the words.

Yet she didn't.

Gideon's arm shook as he stepped towards me. 'They're fighting over buried treasure.'

He pointed the pistol at the others. Sweat dripped off his forehead and into his eyes, the strain rippling through him evident in his desperate attempt to control his body. I was worried the gun would go off by accident.

'What do you want, Gideon?'

I pushed out of the seat. He wiped his arm across his head; it came back wetter than the bottom of the ocean. He forced a smirk through his quivering face.

'I'll do what you and the others have failed to achieve.' His mania reached a high point. 'I'll change history and improve it.'

I looked at Dash. 'We've saved people. Millions are better off because of what we've done, not just here but across the universe.'

He spat on the floor. 'You haven't done enough with the technology you possess. You should have been preventing wars and stopping genocides, not saving the odd kid here and there. Once I get what Gloriana promised me, the rest of the Static and I will change history for the better.' His voice was brittle and rising, fingers trembling on the metal. 'Once we have those Rings adjusted for us, human history will be different.'

It was my turn to laugh, my hands on my sides to stop them from splitting.

'The Rings are useless, Gideon; purely symbolic to help the girls focus their ability during their training.' I grinned at his stupid expression. 'It's all up here.'

I tapped my head as he scowled. Dash inched her way closer to Gideon without him noticing. I was confident she could get the gun from him with her agility.

'What?' he stuttered.

'It's a female-only club in our DNA and our brains. No man will do what we can, never.'

His face was a picture painted by Picasso on a bad day, all parts collapsing into different directions, eyes expanding bigger than his head, lips shrinking in despair while his nose flared like an alcoholic horse. Then he caressed the trigger as an explosion erupted above our heads.

'Shit!' Gideon shouted as Dash fell on him, and he fired at Eighteen. As the bullet squeezed through the air, I hopped through space, reappeared in front of the older version of me, and pushed her to the floor. The slug ripped into my shoulder, pain cutting through my flesh like lightning.

But worse than the wound was the surge of agony rushing through my insides. It wasn't as bad as I'd felt before, probably because I'd only jumped through space and not time, but it was still a hundred daggers digging into my guts.

I fell into the wall as Dash grappled with Gideon.

'Help her,' I said to the other versions of myself. The insides of my stomach were squashed together. I expected everything to burst through my ribs at any second. Sixteen and Seventeen were frozen in shock as Eighteen grabbed my arm and looked at my wound.

'We need to get that fixed,' she said as I watched Dash wrestle the gun from Gideon, and it shot across the floor. He wrapped his hands around Dash's neck as a pirate stumbled through the open door, followed by Ishtar. Anne Bonny clawed at Ishtar's face as they fell onto a table covered in rubbish. Stabs of electricity swam through my bones as blood seeped out of me. Fireworks exploded inside my organs, molten lava replacing the liquid in my veins.

Eighteen pushed her head next to mine. 'Travel to the future, get yourself patched up and return with reinforcements.'

It was a tempting idea, fraught with several dangerous possibilities. The risks were significant, but they were still better than what was unfolding in front of me. Gideon choked the life from Dash as Ishtar smashed a pirate skull against the wall. I searched for the gun in my pocket, but it had disappeared. My fingers moved over the broken glass as I tried to get up.

'Ahhh.' A low rumbling groan spurred out of me as the next wave of agony sped through my organs. I crawled towards Dash as Gideon dug his nails further into her throat. I couldn't do anything for her, for any of them. Not in this condition. My only option was to hop away, recover, and return. Preferably with armed reinforcements.

But if I came back so close to this time, my body would go through the same agony.

I had no choice but to leave.

I searched for the trigger in my head.

Then, before I could imagine being somewhere else, a veil of darkness smothered my brain.

Chapter 16

Fragments

I woke outside, the wind blowing through my hair as I peered at the countryside. The air was crisp and fresh, filled with the sweet scent of wildflowers and the earthy aroma of freshly tilled soil. The distant murmur of cows and the chirping of birds added to the idyllic scene. As the breeze blew through the fields, it carried the pungent smell of hay and the musky perfume of the nearby woods. My guts felt normal again. The pain had disappeared from my shoulder as I reached for the wound, finding it had healed. I wore a clean top, some bizarre design of overlapping material in red and blue.

'The shirt is from the twenty-second century, same for the treatment on your shoulder.'

Gloriana's voice made my neck twitch. A small animal ran over my foot as I rose from the leaves and twigs around me, fingers digging into the wet mud. An electric hum vibrated inside my ears. I scanned the environment, searching for friends, foes, and potential weapons.

'What happened?'

She glanced behind me. 'I got you patched up and saved your pet.'

I turned to see Dash fast asleep in the grass. Gloriana threw something into the shimmering blue light next to her, a sapphire illumination I'd seen before.

'Are we in a time loop?'

The dampness stuck to my fingers, and the bouquet of nature made me think of summer.

'No,' she replied. 'We're on the verge of creating history before changing it beyond recognition.'

The river was ahead of us, near where Dash lay. I strode towards her, never taking my gaze from Gloriana. 'What did you do?'

'Don't worry, they're all okay,' she said.

'All of who?' I said as I reached Dash. As I did, I got the answer to my question. The three older versions of me, Gretel and her Breadcrumbs lay below, in a hollow leading to the water. I checked to see if Dash was okay before moving. All four of them slept. Seeing them slumbering in the grass was bizarre, like staring into a broken mirror. Could I take them from this place one or two at a time, taking the consequences on my body? I would if I had to, but I wanted to know why Gloriana had brought us there.

'There are some marvellous drugs available in this universe.' Gloriana stood next to Dash and peered at me as I got up. 'Unfortunately, there's nothing simple and easy to deal with this.' She tapped her head as I contemplated getting Dash and every version of me away.

'There's something wrong with you?'

I rechecked the area to work out where we were. Large trees surrounded us while the tips of snow-crusted mountains were above them. A swamp was near the river, where insects scuttled across the surface.

'The irony is that none of this would have happened without my illness.'

Gloriana held out her arms and stared at the sleeping versions of me as I inched closer to her. Deep lines were under her eyes, and the sheen had vanished from her skin.

'What's wrong with you?'

She gazed into the trees, seemingly unaware of what I'd said and who else was with her. Then the sparkle returned to her face, and she sprang into life.

'Diana and Ishtar are the most competitive sisters you're ever likely to meet.' She let that nugget of information linger in the air. I still trusted nothing she said. 'That's what drove them to be the best surgeons in the world. They were always striving to get one up on each other, constantly wanting to perform the miracle operation the other couldn't.' Her smile wavered and then disappeared. 'But even together, they couldn't remove the tumour in my head without killing me.' The weight of that swept through her, so she seemed like she was on her last legs.

'You're dying?'

'Oh yes, a slow death has dragged on for hundreds of years, but not for much longer.' She reached into her pocket and found a pill to pop into her mouth.

'So why aren't you dead?'

'Poor Diana, she loved me so much then.'

She looked like she was about to cry until she composed herself and a fierce determination returned to her face.

I wanted to keep her talking. 'Did Diana operate on you?'

Gloriana stared at me. 'She couldn't remove the tumour. Her hand shook with the realisation as she peered into my open skull. I was awake, feeling nothing when her laser scalpel scraped the bottom of my cerebellum. There I was, laid out on the table, thinking of the youth I'd lost when, in an instant, I was back there.'

'You travelled in time?'

'I travelled in time and space. I vanished from that cold operating room in a dying city to fifty years in the past. The sea air shook me out of my haze. I stumbled to the cliff edge and stared at the coast as it was before it became polluted along with the rest of the planet.'

She paused and moved closer. The sheen had disappeared from her skin, replaced with more lines than the surface of Mars.

'It must have scrambled your senses.'

'It was all a dream, that's what I told myself, brought on by the operation and my proximity to death. But it was so real. I tasted the sea air at the back of my throat, felt the wind caress my face, ran the grass through my fingers, and watched the insects scuttle across my shoes.'

'You were inside your past life, visiting your childhood?'

'I took a few minutes to understand that, but yes, I'd travelled far from my disease and the ailing world I lived in.' She bent down and scooped up a fistful of dirt, letting it slip between her fingers and return to the earth. 'I was a dying evolutionary biologist in a fading world. I'd lost all hope, dreaming of my youth again, and then I found it. Or at least I returned to the place where I'd spent it. Then I wished myself back to my present to find a stunned Diana and Ishtar wondering where I'd been for ten minutes.'

'What happened to you?'

She reached out her hand. I didn't flinch. Her fingers were close to mine, but we didn't touch.

'We discovered later that the potential to travel through time and space is connected to female chromosomes and a specific place hidden away at the base of the cerebellum. So all it needed was the removal of a slither of brain matter and visualising where and when you wanted to be.

'Everything that has happened since, with the Watchers and the Queens of Heaven and with you, all came from that point. But there's so much more that needs doing, so many timelines which need saving. And I have to be alive to do it.'

An invisible itch crawled around the scar on my back. 'If the ability is already inside us, inside females, what was the function of the Time Rings?'

'Time travel doesn't apply to all women and girls; it's only a small percentage. We found that the younger they were, the harder it was for them to focus. Diana suggested something for them to concentrate on. That's when I came up with the Rings. Girls like their jewellery.'

Every sinew and membrane in my brain pounded against my skull.

'I saw Ishtar direct Diana to cut into Ursula.' The memory was still vivid. 'Why do that if the ability is already inside us? Why insert the Ring into the body?'

'We had to because young girls can be so... what's the word... rebellious. You're the perfect example of that.' She made my blood boil. 'We needed a tether to stop them vanishing and not returning, an internal tracking device.

That's why I let you slip away, unaware Diana had disabled that facility in the Rings she gave you.'

I lifted my hand, staring at the space where the Time Ring had been for so long.

'You tracked the girls through the Rings?'

'It was for their own good.'

'That's how you knew where Ursula was, that she'd travelled to the Blitz. And then you sent the Static to get her.'

Gloriana shrugged. 'Once the Watchers acquired her, they wiped her mind, but Ursula somehow recalled her true past. I'm unsure if she remembered her parents dying in the Balham Tube Station disaster, but I assume something deep inside Ursula told her to go back there and save them.'

'She's from another planet. I saw her memories.'

Gloriana shook her head. 'Implanted memories. We knew the more we directed what our girls remembered, the more we'd control them. Unfortunately, Ursula's real trauma, the Balham disaster, was problematic in getting her brain to do what we wanted. So Ishtar created false memories, Ursula's childhood problems and the planetary catastrophe. And it worked for a while.'

'You're lying.'

'Gaze into my eyes and see the truth, Ruby.' She looked straight at me. 'And you were so close at Balham when those bombs dropped. You saved her from the bus, but after that....'

An invisible punch knocked the breath from my lungs. A low hum pierced my ears and sent vibrations through every inch of me, screaming down to my chest to crack my ribs and drag my heart out.

'The girl in the road....'

'That was Ursula as a child, yes. It's remarkable that her

brain still contained a memory of that somehow, even after we'd scrubbed her mind clean and replaced it with a much more vivid and vibrant life.'

My legs trembled as I struggled to stay upright. 'If I'd known....'

'Haven't you learnt by now, Ruby, that you can't save everybody? Ursula wasn't the first to slip from our grasp.'

I twisted my hands into fists. 'There were others before me who escaped?'

She turned her lips up in a great pout. 'I would hardly call it an escape. What we offered them, what the Watchers provided, was not a prison. We saved those girls from lives of tyranny and abuse.'

'You experimented on kids!'

I screamed the words at her, the heat in my blood threatening to shoot steam from my mouth. I could have rushed her and dragged her to the river. It wouldn't have taken long to hold her under the water.

She sighed, but didn't look guilty. 'We had to. The results for them and us were too significant not to.'

'And what happened to them all?'

'The strongest became Watchers.'

'And what about the others? What did you do with them?'

Molten lava seethed inside my blood. Yet, outside I was a sea of calm. She waved her fingers at me, dismissing all those kids she had no use for.

'Only the strong survive. There is no room for weakness in our mission.'

I peered into her eyes and found only darkness. I turned my wrists towards her, exposing the marks on them.

'What mission is so important you would sacrifice so many lives?'

'There are always casualties during revolutions, Ruby. Your recent experiences should have taught you that.'

'That was different. Why would you hurt and kill innocents?'

The sadness returned to her face, and I knew it wasn't for me or any of the others.

'Nuclear wars, disease, global pollution, famine, and plague have ravaged my planet, my time. Once I discovered what I could do after my happy surgical accident, Diana, Ishtar and I created the Watchers. Our sole intention was to record all the significant historical events to find which ones we could manipulate to improve our world. Diana thought if we changed too much, we would make things worse; it had to be the correct subtle alterations to save humanity and the planet. So we studied all the history before ours, travelled the universe gathering knowledge from the civilisations we found. Some people believed us to be gods.'

Her arrogance knew no bounds, and she reminded me of me.

'How were you able to travel across space? We need to visualise where we are going.'

She reached into her jacket and removed a device I recognised.

'Do you know what this is, Ruby?'

'Of course – it's a data communicator containing records of every planet and species in the universe. Diana gave me two. It's connected to the Watchers' data storage and updates all the records they make of history.'

'Indeed, and the information changes when time alters.' She grinned at me. 'Have you never wondered how these work and where the original data came from?'

'That's above my pay grade. And I never cared.'

'Do you care now?'

'I guess you're going to tell me either way.'

She pressed the screen, and it flickered into life. I gasped at the sight and clutched my chest, staring at somewhere I knew all too well: Kaladan.

And those who'd become my friends.

'That's Zara Zante and the Yoron.'

They were standing next to the Zante house and the swampland behind it.

'During your recent adventure on Kaladan, did you never ask Zara what she did?'

I shook my head. 'We were rather busy with something else.'

'Ah, yes,' Gloriana said. 'Bringing down the glorious Kaladan Empire. How did that work out?'

I grabbed the device from her, checking the history of Kaladan after the revolution, smiling at what I found.

'Kaladan became a great democracy, eventually founding a new Empire that brought peace and prosperity to the rest of the universe. And they never conquered Earth.'

Relief seeped through me. I'd finally got something right with my meddling in time.

'I can see that makes you happy, Ruby, but you still haven't answered the question of where the Watcher's acquired these devices.'

I peered at the photo on the screen. 'They got them from Kaladan?' She nodded. 'With all the information already stored on them.'

'Yes, a universe full of data installed on the machines by Zara Zante. You inspired her, Ruby. Her life's' work was using her skills to program them with all the planetary locations the Watchers needed to travel through space. By the time the Kaladan delegation reached Earth, they left one of the devices behind, where Ishtar retrieved it.'

'How did Zara obtain the original data?' I said. 'There were only seven planets in the Kaladan Empire when I left them.'

Gloriana shook her head. 'You still don't get it, do you, Ruby? Zara got all the details from the Yoron. And who did they receive it from?'

The quivering returned to my legs, and I had to place one hand on a tree to stop from falling over. The bark nipped at my fingers and switched a light bulb on in my head.

'From me. The Yoron got it from me.'

'Yes. From what I understand, it wasn't deliberate. They didn't go peering through your brain for your secrets, but somehow the information must have filtered into the minds of every Yoron you transported across Kaladan that day of the revolution. Your perfect memory dribbled into theirs. So then, after you'd left the planet, Zara Zante – a prominent Kaladanian zoologist – worked closely with the Yoron to record their history and customs. That's when they revealed to her what they'd discovered from you. And Zara knew the data was too important to lose, so she recorded it for posterity.'

'But... that means I caused a temporal paradox. None of what's happened would have occurred without me going to Kaladan and causing the revolution. And I was only there to remove the communication device from my head, which wouldn't have been there if I hadn't needed to communicate with Ursula to find where the Queens of Heaven were holding Diana prisoner. And....'

I closed my eyes, unable to return to the temporal para-

135

dox's starting point. When I reopened them, Gloriana grinned at me.

'See, isn't changing time exciting? I told the Watchers we must do this to save our planet.'

A shiver trembled through my spine. 'But it didn't work, did it?'

Her grin vanished as the darkness under her eyes increased. 'Under my guidance, the Watchers took the information from the database the Kaladanians had left on Earth and travelled in time to record human history. They didn't realise it, but I searched for those points that could be altered to save our future. Then it was the Queens of Heaven's responsibility to make the changes, but nothing helped: our nuclear destiny was still there. But we thought, with time, we would find the right solution. Then we discovered we weren't immortal. We are still ageing, only slower than normal.' The weight of eternity consumed her voice. 'Nothing alters that ultimate nuclear outcome. All we did was create fragments of the original timeline and parallel realities.'

I moved away from her. 'Tell me about the fragments.'

A flock of birds flew above us, tiptoeing across the landscape.

'You mean if a person travelled into the past and killed their grandparents, would they disappear?'

'That's one thing I've yet to try,' I said. 'If only I knew who my grandparents were.'

Gloriana turned and walked to the river's edge. I glanced at Dash, who slumbered in the grass. There was enough distance between Gloriana and me to grab Dash and leave. The idea flashed through my mind before I followed her to the river.

'Changing the past does nothing for that future.'

Gloriana picked up a stone. She threw it across the water and watched the ripples follow the object before disappearing. 'All they do is create an alternative future without that version of themselves, but they and their reality still exist. You found this out with Daisy.'

The memory of Daisy's scarred face hit the front of my brain. Then it changed to the news report of her death. But, if what she said was true, I hadn't altered those moments. A thin mist drifted off the top of the river and floated towards me. Gloriana was just out of my view, my gaze peering at the troubled reflection flickering in the water.

'You're saying you can never change this nuclear wasteland you come from?'

Gloriana knelt and gazed into the river. She dipped her hand into the surface and swirled it around her liquid echo.

'That future can't be changed using the measures the Queens have tried. So I told them this, explained to Ishtar that we needed a more powerful solution if we were to be Queens of all we survey.'

She was an enigma wrapped in a riddle. 'This is all so you can pursue your grand plan of saving humanity?'

Gloriana arched her eyebrows. 'Why wouldn't we want to do that? How many times have you saved lives by changing time? What is it that drives you to do such things?'

'I haven't gone out of my way to kill people to do it.'

The terrible image of those brains burning inside the loop generator seared my skull, the aroma of waiting death still infusing my senses from the hospital in Nagasaki. And the thought of all the kids she and the others had experimented on and used.

My words were meaningless to her.

'We've tried manipulating all the key points' throughout

human history, but nothing changes the outcome. So it's time for something more dramatic.'

'Which is what?'

She seemed surprised by my question, as if I hadn't been paying attention all along. Gloriana moved from the water and headed towards the brazier with the shimmering blue light. She placed her hand above it.

'We need as much time energy as possible to pursue the most extreme measure of changing the history of this planet, an alteration so significant there will be no more fragments.'

I glanced over at the other versions of myself. 'Why are they here? Why do they even exist? What happened to the first fourteen years of my life?'

She touched the edge of the blue light, and sparks jumped from it. 'Have your memories returned?'

I hesitated with my reply, fascinated by how the flashes settled onto her skin. A bouquet of burnt flesh drifted through the air.

'Not enough of them.'

'Then I shall tell you some of them. Would you like that?'

This is what I'd searched for all these years, what I'd dreamt about every night. I nodded as butterflies invaded my heart.

'Go ahead.'

Chapter 17

Ruby's Diary

Day Eight Hundred and Two, Year Three

E arth Time: 2232. Location: Kostuk. (Planet Pegula).
The early morning news sent a chill through my heart. I left the screen on and went outside, banging on Elizabeth's door.

'Turn on the TV,' I said when she let me in.

Charles sat in the corner, eyes glazed over, mind wandering into some twilight land of confusion and despair. Elizabeth turned on the set before sitting next to her husband and gripping his hand.

'Who are you?' he said to her.

She refused to look dismayed at his question and continued to hold his fingers. Tears formed in his eyes, his voice wavering as he looked between her and me as Elizabeth found the right channel.

'Everything's okay, Charles.'

'Who are you? What have you done with my wife? Where's Elizabeth?'

Elizabeth reached behind her and retrieved a watercolour painting of a garden. She handed it to him.

'We got married in that garden,' he said.

It must have come from somewhere deep in his memory. He ran his fingers across the thin sheen of dust on the glass, brushing away the haze obscuring his past life. He gazed at it as the TV sprang into life. I recognised the red and black logo of the PHA, the government's Public Health Announcements. Elizabeth held Charles's hand as he continued to stare at the frame.

The presenter betrayed no emotion as she spoke.

The following changes are effective immediately throughout the general population. WELLBORN is compulsory nationwide. This is a list of facilities that will carry out the procedure.

I watched the names of the sterilisation centres and abortion clinics swim over the screen. My stomach churned at the thought of those who would endure this. All those deemed by the State to be mentally or physically unable to be mothers or fathers.

'That is terrible, Ruby, but....'

'Wait,' I said.

The Mercy Sleep is compulsory across the nation. This is a list of facilities that will carry out the procedure.

Elizabeth gasped as the broadcast finished, and the screen changed to an old cartoon of a frustrated cat trying to kill a tiny mouse. Elizabeth's legs gave way, and I caught her before she fell. I lifted her, and she wriggled out of my hands.

'They won't get away with it; people will protest,' she said.

My short time living and working on Pegula made me doubt that.

'I don't think they will, Elizabeth.'

She glanced at her husband. 'As long as they don't know Charles is here, we'll be fine. I'll keep him inside.'

I shook my head. 'You're forgetting the drone at the party.'

Elizabeth put a hand to her face as somebody banged on the door. She let them bang again, louder this time and more assertive, watching Charles as he stared at a giant black spider crawling across the carpet. She stopped him before he could scoop up those eight legs and plop the unfortunate arachnid into his mouth. She deposited it on the window ledge as I looked outside to see who was there.

The banging returned. 'Open up. This is the State Patrol.'

I couldn't see them, but a large green bus was parked on the road with all its windows painted over. I saw only part of the registration plate, which said T4. Before Elizabeth could respond, Charles walked over and opened the door.

'Elizabeth and Charles Marx?' He was dressed in a military uniform with a pistol strapped to his waist. Behind him stood two others with rifles over their shoulders. He handed Elizabeth a piece of paper with an official State stamp at the top.

'What is this?' I said.

He glared at me. 'Who are you?'

'A friend.'

His glare intensified. 'This doesn't concern you. Step aside.' He turned to Elizabeth. 'We're here to collect Charles Marx. We need your signature. This explains everything.' He handed her a data memory stick.

'I don't have a computer,' she said.

There was nothing behind his eyes as he stared at her. He placed his hand on her shoulder, and for one second, I thought he'd offer sympathy or condolences, but he pushed her to the side and marched over to Charles. He gazed at something on his communicator before staring at the scared-looking man in the corner.

'Take him away,' he commanded the other two. They came in together, restraints hanging from both sets of hands. I wanted to scream, shout, and beat them mercilessly with my fists. But I did nothing.

Elizabeth spoke. 'Take me with you.'

Charles whimpered as they put the handcuffs on him.

'We're only here for him.' He had a voice sculpted from frost. He walked outside, his people following him, dragging a distraught and terrified Charles with them.

Elizabeth strode after the commander and placed her hand on his arm. 'Take me with you; with him.'

'We can't....'

'I have what he has, the same disease.'

The female soldier with the red hair peeking out from underneath her cap spoke. 'It'll save us returning to this craphole.' The other one, the leader, narrowed his gaze and peered deep into Elizabeth.

'There is no medical record of your deficiency. We have no orders relating to you.' He turned his back on her as the others bundled Charles into the bus. Elizabeth stood there, and I went to her, glimpsing frightened eyes lurking in the shadows inside the vehicle. They threw Charles to the floor and shut the door behind him. All I saw was the fear on his face as Elizabeth collapsed and the dirty green bus pulled away.

I helped her up. 'Let's go inside, Elizabeth.'

None of the neighbours offered help, scattering to the safety of their homes.

'I failed him,' Elizabeth said.

My arm was in hers as I helped her inside, closing the door behind us. She slumped in my arms and sobbed.

I stood there, helpless.

Then I took her to bed, sleeping on the sofa and never leaving her place.

When I woke, she was gone, with a note on the table.

I'll prove to them I'm ill. Then they'll have to put me with Charles.

I reread it before stepping outside. The sun beat down on my face, and I didn't cover my eyes. The neighbours ignored me as they went about their business, and the note felt like a death in my hands. I peered at the words and considered how I could help Elizabeth and Charles.

Go back in time and prevent his dementia? That was impossible. Stop the State Patrol from going to the flat? That was beyond me. Could I foil that drone from recording what happened at the party? It would be easier to convince Elizabeth to keep George home that day. And I wasn't even sure that was how they found out about him. It was more likely because of the trip I convinced her to take to the doctor.

So perhaps I was to blame, interfering where I shouldn't have.

What could I do?

Nothing. There was nothing I could do to keep Elizabeth and George together.

I turned my hand into a fist and looked at the Time Ring.

What good was it if I couldn't save lives?

That was when I knew what to do with the rest of my life.

My missing past wasn't important.

Other people's futures were.

Chapter 18

The Memories of Time

'When you were six, you fell onto some glass and cut your knee; you still have the scar. Your father gazed at you as if you were stupid; your mother cleaned the wound, exhibiting no emotion. It is the first memory you have of your life.'

Pain shot through my knee as she spoke. The memory was there; I could touch it, could remember the sensation of the glass slicing into me. Yet, that reminiscence wasn't there sixty seconds ago.

'One year later was your first day at school. You saw your coat hanging in the cloakroom; your mother had written your name on the collar. You were all alone, surrounded by other kids but consumed by isolation. You didn't want to stay there, but you couldn't go home. You wanted to die.'

An abyss of loneliness surged through me, biting at my limbs and creating a weight heavier than the sun. I wanted to fall to the ground and climb into the dirt.

'At eight years old, you discovered your love of music when you found a long-lost recording of the Supremes on some obscure part of the computer network. You wanted to be Florence Ballard; you dreamed of being a singer, but your only friends were countless women and girls dead to history.'

Dizziness hit me, and my legs buckled as I flopped onto the grass. All I thought about was buttered popcorn. Then, at the rear of my skull, a lilting voice sang.

'When you were ten, your mother threw herself from the cliffs, and your father blamed you. It was the only time he showed any emotion. The whip marks have left your skin, but they still linger in the corners of your mind.'

A fire burnt into my back in long strips, one lash after another, as the smell of my seared flesh ravaged my senses. I clawed at the ground, damp mud crawling over my fingers.

'Do you want to learn more about those first fourteen years of your life?'

I stared right through her and turned to ice. 'How... how... do you know...?'

Her hands were on mine before I could move away. She pulled me up.

'I know all this because your missing memories are

mine, Ruby. Diana thought it best to remove them when she plucked you from the timeline. It's the same with the other versions of me.'

She twisted her head to Gretel and the Breadcrumbs as I went numb. I wanted to squirm from her grip, but I knew my legs would give way and collapse again if I did.

'This... this can't be true.'

'It wasn't my idea; Diana came up with it.' She smiled as my guts churned, a whirlpool of spasms hitting every part of me. 'Diana theorised that collecting time energy from alternate younger variants of me could cure my tumour. I was overjoyed when she explained it, but nothing could remedy my illness. Then I realised there could be other benefits to plucking versions of me from my past.'

Her hand was in mine, and I left it there. 'What benefits?'

'Other versions of me, younger copies of me, would provide the power to allow me to jump to the beginning of humanity and make the modifications required to prevent the nuclear future. So we took five forms of me from my timeline, starting backwards from when I was eighteen. Diana trained you and the others separate from each other.' She sighed heavily. 'And then there was an unfortunate accident with the fifteen-year-old version of me, which led to Diana having doubts about what I'd proposed. That is when she helped you escape and hid those other three somewhere in time.'

I pushed her away. My knees buckled, and I staggered to the side, my hand reaching for the closest tree. The bark was sharp and nipped my fingers, the world spinning around me, nausea infecting my throat and lungs.

'I'm... I'm you? So what Ishtar told me is true?'

Gloriana inched over. 'Ishtar needed you as much as I did, all because of what Diana hid deep inside your head.'

My nails cut into my palm, the pain bringing clarity to my mind. It didn't matter what she said; I wouldn't give her anything.

'Those memories are gone; there's nothing there to help you.'

Her shadow crept toward me. The wind howled through my ears even though the weather was calm.

'Diana agreed with me about collecting some of our fragments. She started this whole thing because she was keen to interact with a younger version of herself.'

Blood dripped from my fingers and across the marks on my wrist.

'There's a fragment of Diana somewhere?'

Gloriana's hand was on the tree as I slumped below her. I wanted to be anywhere but there, too tired to reach the trigger in my mind.

'Diana always craved to be a mother, and this was the closest she could get to that. Then she panicked and got the wrong idea about me and the experiments. She didn't want me to have the kid. So Diana took her away and placed her somewhere in time, hiding the location inside your head. That is why I had to manipulate you into finding her.'

Gloriana moved to the side, towards the shimmering blue light. There was a shape behind her feet, the shadow of a child.

'What did you do?'

'As soon as I discovered Diana's betrayal, I scoured all the data we had on you and discovered your obsession with changing time and saving lives. And that's when I left a trail of breadcrumbs for you to pursue and me to follow.'

'What breadcrumbs?' Fear possessed me.

'It took me a long time; little details dripped all over time and space until everything fell into place high above Earth's moon. First, I whispered into Elric Oban's ear about the Watchers. I told him a rogue child was hiding from them, and she was the one who would return his wife to him. I even gave him the idea about the lizardmen and the anti-matter engine. Then I placed a self-thinking, mobile electronic device inside the engine you left at your hide-away below Stonehenge.'

A thousand blazing suns collapsed onto me. 'You've been spying on me all this time?'

If only I'd stored the anti-matter engine away like I said I would to Dash.

'I'm the original Watcher, Ruby. All I've done is record your experiences. And then you led me to the other versions of us and the one of Diana.'

The knot tightened around my heart. I moved forward and stared down at the dozing body behind Gloriana.

'Daisy!'

'Diana was feisty when she was younger, wasn't she?'

My head spun, pain shooting through my guts and into my brain. 'If you've hurt her....'

'Don't be silly. I could have taken her earlier but I needed her, you and the others all together for the energy container. Five should be enough for what I require.'

'My first meeting with Daisy on the pier; how did that happen?' A weapon. I needed a weapon.

'Diana is not only skilled at removing memories. She planted a trigger inside your head, a word to send you to the location where Daisy was. Unfortunately for the both of you, I tricked it out of Diana before she realised what she'd done.'

There were so many holes in my heart I expected every fibre of me to leak out.

'I don't believe you.'

'Why? Because it sounds umpossible?'

A succession of meteors crashed against my insides. 'That word; it was all because of you?'

She shook her head. 'It was Diana's plan for getting you and the girl together once she separated you from me. It took me three centuries to embed umpossible into the Zardoz language.' She wiped an insect from her arm in disgust. 'It wasn't pleasant, I can tell you, but it was worth it. Diana grew up along the same part of the coast we did. She couldn't help but drop the kid off there. Such a shame her face got messed up by that lunatic father of hers.'

I remembered the crimes of Dale Lynx. I recalled the love of Lucy Lynx for her daughter.

'Daisy can't be a younger version of Diana. I've met her mother.' And I'd drugged Dale Lynx and framed him for a crime he didn't commit.

Gloriana picked up the slumbering child, Daisy's head close to that blue fire.

'Diana is an expert at manipulating memories, particularly with the skills we gained during our many trips to Kaladan. It would have been easy for her to get all three to believe they were a family, and electronic records are so simple to manipulate.'

Her words washed over me, and my eyes fixed on Daisy's vulnerable body. Did I believe any of what she'd said?

'You, the Watchers, and the Queens have done your damnedest to change your future and failed every time. So what makes you think collecting time energy from me and the others will make a difference now?'

'Look around, Ruby, cast your mind back across all your trips through human history. Who is always the instigator of cruel and terrible events?'

I shrugged, trying to figure out how I'd stop whatever mad scheme she'd planned.

'I don't know what you mean.'

'The male of the species has created all the world's worst problems. It's them we have to deal with.'

I laughed in her face. 'Good luck with that.'

'Do you think it's a coincidence only women can travel through time and space?'

'It's a genetic anomaly.'

She scoffed at the suggestion. 'No, this is an evolution in action; Mother Nature is rectifying her mistake. I'm unsure if the ability was always there or if our DNA changed over time to adapt to our many injustices.' A fanatic's devotion burned in her face. 'Human evolution is a lengthy process of change. Scientific evidence shows that all people's physical and behavioural traits originated from apelike ancestors and evolved over approximately six million years.'

I scanned my surroundings, still searching for something to use as a weapon.

'This is all fascinating, Gloriana, but Diana taught me this long ago.'

'Good. I hope you were paying attention. Three significant revolutions mark the history of life on Earth. The first was life itself, sometimes before 3.5 billion years ago. Life, in the form of microorganisms, became a powerful force in a world where previously only chemistry and physics had operated. The second revolution was the origin of multicellular organisms about half a billion years ago. Life became complex as plants and animals of myriad forms and sizes evolved and interacted in fertile ecosystems. The origin of human consciousness was the third event sometime within the last 2.5 million years. Life became aware of itself and transformed the world of nature to its own ends.

'But there was still a long gap between then and the development of our ancestors: *Homo sapiens*, the first modern humans, evolved from their early hominid predecessors between 200,000 and 300,000 years ago. They developed a capacity for language about 50,000 years ago, and the first modern humans began moving outside Africa about 70,000-100,000 years ago.' Her eyes shone as she spoke. 'I know Diana will have taught you all this because she was fascinated with not just human evolution but the evolution of language.'

'The evolution of language?'

'Yes. The power we have in our brains, even in ordinary, normal human brains, would be nothing without language. The force that seems to have accelerated our brain's growth is a new kind of stimulant: language, signs, collective memories – all elements of culture. As our cultures evolved in complexity, so did our brains, which drove our cultures to greater complexity. Big and clever brains led to more complex civilisations, leading to bigger and smarter brains.

'Spoken language clearly differentiates *Homo sapiens* from all other creatures. None but humankind produces a complex spoken language, a medium for communication and a medium for introspective reflection. The brain of *Homo sapiens* is three times the size of the brain of our nearest evolutionary relatives, the African great apes.' She tapped the side of her head. 'You must have seen it with your experiments, especially on the creature from Felineous. Our ability to travel through time and space is an evolutionary change in our female brains. But, unfortunately, it came too late and in too few of us to prevent the nuclear Armageddon in my time. That has to change for our species to survive.'

'So you intend to go back to the dawn of human evolution and do what — wipe out male chromosomes?'

'That's one option but too extreme, even for me.' There was a glint in her eye. 'I need not to change men, but change us.'

'Us?'

'I have to modify female DNA. We must be stronger than them, not physically, but here.' She touched her head.

'You want to make them dumber than us? I don't think you need to adjust history to do that.' I allowed myself to grin.

'As much as I like the idea of lobotomising most men through time, they'd still be physically stronger than most of us. So no, I'm going to travel back and alter female DNA, so we're better than them.'

'Better in what way?'

'It's simple. I'll alter evolutionary biology so all females will have telekinetic abilities. No man will be stronger than a woman ever again.'

She seemed proud of her plan, but all I thought about was a brave young woman on an alien planet far from me in space and time.

'What did you do when you visited Kaladan?'

'What did I do? I found the only telekinetics in the universe and examined their brains. But unfortunately, the Yoron physiology was too alien for me to use, so I visited the girl who saved your life on Kaladan, Dr Zante's descendant. The second Zara Zante was useful in helping me understand what I needed to do. It's a shame I had to slice her up.'

Invisible fingers reached down my throat, found their

way into my chest and wrapped themselves around my heart. And then they squeezed.

It took me a minute before I could speak.

'You intend to inject Kaladanian DNA into the beginnings of humanity?'

'Yes, and it will only alter the female chromosomes.'

A cluster of tiny bombs exploded inside my abdomen. Rage filled me up like rainwater in an empty well.

I needed to keep it under control. 'You don't understand what injecting alien cells into human DNA might do; you could wipe out our species, maybe damage human biology beyond repair.'

Gloriana ignored my words. 'It's worth the risk. I only need to hop back in time, about 300,000 years.'

I wouldn't admit it to her, but what she'd said fascinated me. Yet now I knew it was an impossible dream; or an unimaginable nightmare.

'You can't do that. Diana told me the Watchers can only travel so far in time, and it's nowhere near 300,000 years.' The furthest I'd gone was 5,000 years when I commissioned the builders of Frixion Prime to create the base under Stonehenge. 'We don't have the power to travel that far.'

She beamed at me. 'And now you understand why I need the time energy from Daisy and the rest of you.'

I stared at the three versions of me, then Daisy, reminding myself that what Gloriana proposed wasn't possible. 'How do you think this will work?'

'You observed how the combined energy in a group of normal human brains created a loop?'

'I saw how your renegade Watchers, your so-called Queens of Heaven, killed people for your obscene experiments.'

She shifted her body as Daisy snored in her arms. 'I

think you forget how all our tests started with Diana.' She laid Daisy at the foot of the brazier. 'That woman may well be the greatest genius in history. Once we pulled the versions of me from the past, she theorised that the particular time energy inside my brain, if it was syphoned off and stored with the energy from my younger selves, could be combined to cure my tumour or even stop the ageing process. Of course, both results were futile, but I had another idea.'

'You want to use the energy to travel back 300,000 years for this crazed plan?'

She laughed at me. 'You realise it could work, Ruby. You are me, so you must know.'

'Don't you need an outside energy source to power it up, to boost it through the ignition phase?'

'See, I knew you were as clever as me. Do you know what year this is?'

She took something from her pocket and dropped it into the blue flame. It had been on the point of fizzling out, but sparked back into action. I studied the environment again. There was no sign of any other living thing. I peered into the sky, searching for birds, but it was empty, apart from a strange tingle in the air. Life had abandoned this place.

'I don't know where we are.'

'I think even nature knows what's coming,' Gloriana said.

'This could be anytime.'

I turned back to where Daisy lay. I could push Gloriana out of the way, grab Daisy and hop away in time or space. But that would mean leaving Dash and the others. If I returned to this point, the shock would cripple me, just like it did in the Blitz Club.

I had to find another solution.

'It's 1908, Siberia,' Gloriana said.

A cold wind swept above my head, the silence echoing inside my skull. 'This is Tunguska?'

She checked something on her communicator. 'And we have about twenty minutes to impact. That's enough time for my friends to slice out all your brains.'

I turned from her and ran straight into the pirates.

Chapter 19

The Big Bang

Pirate arms grappled me to the ground. Anne Bonny was on one side, Mary Read on the other. My neck bent forward, eyes peering at the ants crawling at my feet. There was an electric buzz in the air, the aroma of the blue flame reminding me of fried bananas.

I struggled against them, my instincts telling me to fight when I could have flicked the trigger in my head to escape. But then I couldn't return for three minutes without paralysing my body. And it would have been too late by then – Gloriana would have killed the others to kick-start her mad plan to travel to the dawn of human evolution.

And change it. Or destroy it.

I pushed against the pirates as they dragged me up, Bonny and Read holding my arms with strength greater than mine.

'You can come out now, Nettie.'

Gloriana's voice drifted over me and towards the trees at my side. One pirate grabbed my hair and thrust my head up, forcing me to stare at the person striding forwards.

I spoke through gritted teeth. 'Let go of me.'

Gloriana grinned at me. 'Ruby, this is Nettie. I believe you two have already met.'

The woman from the hospital approached me with her hand out as if she wanted me to shake it. The pirates loosened their grip on my shoulders, but I was in no mood to greet any of these lunatics.

'You were the one who warned me against Gloriana. Was that another deception?'

'People change their minds all the time, Ruby. And when you've lived as long as I have, there are fluctuations in your path. Once you rejected me on Kaladan, I knew you were too stubborn to work with.' She leant closer to me. 'If you'd listened to me, none of this would have happened.'

Her gestures were as empty as her words, flicking her eyelids at me as if she'd just stepped out of a movie screen.

Gloriana strode forwards. 'Nettie is the foremost geneticist we have, and the team she assembled has worked wonders with the Kaladanian DNA we acquired.'

Heat consumed my cheeks as I scowled at the woman with the scarred hands.

'Is that why you were on Kaladan, to experiment on its people?'

Nettie shrugged. 'Not just its population, but the Yoron as well. But their biology proved too alien for us to use, so I took what you'd told the Zantes about their descendant and travelled into Kaladan's future.' Her eyes shimmered as she spoke. 'I watched from a distance as she saved you from that falling building. You were on the ground, dazed from a laser gun wound to your temple, unable to teleport away from impending death, when Zara Zante used her mind to lift you to safety. And it was such a helpful mind.'

'What did you do to her?'

She ignored my question as Gloriana placed her fingers on my cheek, stroking my face and making my flesh crawl.

'I'd forgotten how smooth my skin was.'

I flexed my arms against the pirates and glared at her. 'Those lines on your face are getting thicker by the day. Now tell me what you did to Zara.'

'She doesn't matter. There's still time for me to achieve my goal.' She gripped my chin and squeezed. 'Imagine a world where all women and girls can control things with their minds.'

Her hand lingered on me, disgust shivering through my bones. I liked the idea, but not at this cost, not with her in charge. Sometimes I hated myself, but this was something different. There was a reason why a telekinetic ability was rare in the females of Kaladan.

'The DNA which causes telekinesis kills or deforms fifty per cent of Kaladanian females. So, do you really want to take that risk with humans?'

Nettie looked at me. 'The tests have gone well, but I'm not sure if we're ready to....'

Gloriana cut Nettie short with a wave of her hand. 'We do it now. No more waiting. A fifty per cent success rate is better than nothing.' She ran her fingers across her cheeks. 'I don't know how long I have left.'

'You could always suck our brains out and feed on that to make you younger,' I said as the pirates dragged me over the grass. I scowled at Gloriana; my vision focused on where Dash slumbered. If they'd gotten the dose wrong for her feline biology, there was a chance she could wake sooner than they expected. And Dash was a ferocious fighter when angry.

'Is the container ready?' Gloriana asked my captors.

Mary Read let go of my arm and removed the bag from her shoulder. 'It's in here with the syringe, Your Highness.'

I burst out laughing. 'Your Highness?'

Gloriana stared at me. 'Every society needs a hierarchy to function properly.'

'You sound like Isabella Vale, the former Empress of the Kaladan Empire. A hierarchy I helped crush.'

'Yes, and look where that got you.'

My heart sank. She was right – removing Isabella and destroying her Empire had caused the temporal paradox that had led us all here.

This was all my fault.

But I couldn't think like that; instead, focusing on the madwoman in front of me.

The mad version of me.

'I know you call your little cult the Queens of Heaven, but that is beyond arrogance.'

While I laughed, I assessed the situation to see if I could evade Anne Bonny. After that, it would be a case of battling through the rest as I couldn't escape with Dash, Daisy, and the others. I didn't like the odds.

Gloriana took the bag from Mary Read, removing a large needle.

'I could tell you this won't hurt, but that would be a lie. It will be easier on the others since they're in the land of Nod, but it won't be comfortable for you.'

She handed the implement to Nettie.

I puffed out my cheeks. 'None of this can work.'

She ignored me. 'It will go right into the end of the cerebellum, where Diana chipped a bit away from you all those years ago. Then it will be one long suck to remove the energy we need.' She rechecked her communicator. 'There should be enough time before the explosion to complete the process on all five of you. Nettie will do you last, so you can watch it happen to the others.'

'How do you know there'll be a blast?'

The sight of the syringe didn't worry me; it made me happy. It would make an excellent weapon if I got it away from Nettie.

Gloriana arched her eyebrows. 'Is the stress scrambling that perfect memory of yours? One of the largest explosions ever recorded in human history will occur on this spot in about twenty minutes.'

The strength returned to my body, and my mind was calm and focused on what I needed to do.

'I know there'll be a blast here, but even after all the studies of the Tunguska event, nobody is sure what actually happened. So maybe when you stick that syringe into one of our brains and syphon off the time energy, it causes the explosion history has recorded took place here.'

She shook her head before looking up. 'The airburst of a meteoroid will disintegrate the rock about five miles above us soon, so we need to get on with this. Nettie, start with the teenage versions of me over there.'

The geneticist didn't move, so I took it as a cue to keep talking.

'That theory is one of many suppositions about the blast. Have you never considered that butchering us and placing the time energy into the container and that weird blue flame could cause the explosion?' She gazed at me as if I was the stupid version of her. I was on a roll. 'When you're standing near that brazier, you look like witches plotting around a cauldron.'

As Gloriana glared in my direction, Nettie retrieved me from Anne Bonny. She smiled as the sharp end of the syringe glistened in the light. The pirates joined their leader as they towered above Daisy. They spoke amongst themselves and ignored me.

'You could leave here anytime you want,' Nettie said. 'So why don't you?'

I scowled at her. 'I won't abandon my friends.'

She glanced at them. 'And the other versions of you, of course. There's too many of them to take with you, even if you could get through Gloriana's pirates.'

'And you,' I said. 'I'd have to fight you.'

Nettie loosened her grip on me. 'No, you don't. If I look after your friends, will you handle Gloriana?'

There was an opportunity to snatch the needle from her, but I didn't.

'Handle her how?'

Nettie leaned in close to my face. Her breath was warm on my skin, her perfume as sweet as sugar.

'She's a fanatic. She'll do anything to change that world of hers. But you won't talk her out of her mission, and you can't lock her up. You need something more final to end her threat to humankind.' Her voice quivered next to my cheek; the fear in her words was tangible. 'The alien DNA will corrupt humanity at its birth. But none of it will transform her future or ours.'

'Which side are you on?' I trusted her as much as any of them.

'Does it matter if I save your friends?'

'Can I depend on you?'

'What choice do you have?'

I contemplated her offer as Gloriana and the pirates looked at Daisy and the other versions of me. Bonny and Read walked towards Daisy. Gloriana grinned at me as they reached for the kid, the syringe glistening in the electric air. Life swept out of me in a rush, my chest contracting. They picked Daisy up and moved towards their leader.

Nettie let go of my arm. She was correct; it didn't matter. I had no other options available. They were twenty feet away. Gloriana pointed the syringe at Daisy's neck as I hopped two seconds into the future. I landed on top of the four of them. Pain shot through my stomach as we tumbled to the ground. Daisy rolled to one side as atomic bombs erupted inside me. I wrapped my arms around them, pushing through the agony to hop again. We hit the beach in the eighteenth-century Bahamas. A thousand tiny daggers jigged across my brain. I let go of Bonny and Read; fingers gripped into Gloriana's palm as I hopped onto Salt-burn cliffs in the middle of the twenty-first century. The strain on her face echoed what was coursing through my veins.

My vision disappeared amidst a swirl of blurred mist; every sinew in my body was on fire. I didn't have enough strength to scream, but the noise erupted inside my head. Gloriana slipped from my hand and lay next to me. An invisible weight pushed me into the grass. Moisture from the sea covered my face and swam into my mouth and nose. The breath fell from my throat. As Gloriana called out my name, death would have been preferable to what I was enduring. Whiplash spread through me like molten lava as the gods hammered on every bone.

I was helpless to stop Gloriana. I twisted to look at her, my eyes struggling to see what was around me. We'd landed on a slope. I clutched at my stomach and threw up. Then Gloriana rolled away. She bowled towards the cliff edge and the hundred-foot drop to the sea. Ghostly hands clawed at my insides as I waited for her to use her ability to escape from the danger rushing at her.

But she didn't.

Something was wrong.

Was she unconscious? Did I knock her out when we'd hit the ground in the Caribbean?

All I had to do was lay there in pain and watch her disappear. That would be the finality Nettie wanted. Every part of me throbbed as if plugged into an electricity socket. Tears engulfed my face as Gloriana vanished over the edge. This was it; this was my chance to end her plans.

All I had to do was let her die.

Chapter 20

The Test of Time

I couldn't do it. I couldn't let her die.

I hopped again, reappearing over the edge, falling through a group of startled birds, feathers crashing into my eyes and flesh. I caught Gloriana's arm. The sea was below us, the waves roaring against the beach. But it wouldn't be that way for long. We sped towards it. The wind battered my face as my mind shrunk near to blacking out. No part of me was devoid of agony. Maybe it would be best if we both went out like this. I thought of Dash. And then of Daisy. Then Diana.

All the Ds.

Everything but Death.

One last time I reached into my brain, and we disappeared again.

We hit the wooden flooring of the pier, splinters of timber thrusting into my side and legs. I had no life left in me, my eyes on the verge of closing. I wasn't far from where I'd met Daisy with the scarred face playing with her friends. The last thing I saw was a giant white bird nibbling at my fingers.

* * *

When I came around, I threw up a vast, gut-wrenching spew over the side of the pier. It was as if someone had thrust hands down my throat and into my stomach before dragging everything out. It tasted of blood and bile.

'That looks painful.'

Gloriana stared at me as I rolled to my side. Death would have been preferable to this.

'You have no idea,' I croaked.

'I've never done successive quick time jumps like that. Diana was the first to do it, and I saw its effects on her. It wasn't pretty, but it appears worse for you. We could never work out why time jumps so close to each other would do that to the body.'

'You're welcome.'

The words crawled out of my mouth, my throat burning hotter than the sun. Every knife in existence was sticking into my organs.

'I'm guessing it was Nettie who facilitated your escape. I hope you realise you can't trust her.'

'She saved me from the decapitation you planned.'

I dug my nails into the wood and crawled from the edge. Focusing on her might help me ignore the turmoil running through my flesh and bones.

Gloriana scrunched the muscles in her face. 'Don't be silly; we wouldn't chop your head off. Just pull out some of the time energy in your brain. And as for Nettie: she worked for the Watchers, then she worked for the Queens, then she worked for Ishtar, then threw her hat in with me, and now she's helping you; when all along she's only been working for herself.'

I pushed up, leaning against the rail and breathing slowly. 'It doesn't matter. Your plans are ruined.'

She stared at the sea, her gaze fixed on the horizon. She had nothing to fear from me while my crippled body was on the floor.

'Why? I could easily take you back to Tunguska and start again in your current state.'

'The others won't be there.'

I crawled across the pier like a slug. She flicked her eyelids at me and sighed. God, I hoped the others wouldn't be there. I didn't want to have gone through all the torture for nothing.

'My future looks so different from this.' She pointed down at the sand and the sea. 'There is no blue in the water, no orange in the sand. All that you survey is dark and irradiated. Poison lingers in the air. Nothing living can exist there anymore. Ninety per cent of the planet is the same.' She turned back to me, tears in her eyes. 'We tried to change it so many times. Diana wouldn't contemplate violence, but there was nothing Ishtar and I wouldn't do to prevent that apocalyptic world from happening.'

Giant invisible hands squeezed my body, my bones and

organs pushed together, but I focused my mind on her. 'What caused this nuclear holocaust?'

'How do all wars begin?' Sadness dripped from her eyes. 'A group of men in one country couldn't get what they wanted from another group in a second country, and they pressed buttons to pacify fragile masculinity. So Ishtar and I travelled back five years before that point and removed the leaders of both countries.'

She allowed me to digest her words.

'How did you remove them?'

Gloriana twisted her neck to stare into the sky. 'What do you think we did?'

'You killed them.'

'I would kill one to save ten, so killing two to save millions was easy.' She ran her fingers across her head. 'Getting this tumour was fate. That's what led to Diana's scalpel slipping inside my skull, to us discovering some women and girls had this amazing ability in them all along.'

The internal heat dissipated from me as a sense of control returned to my brain and my limbs. 'I'm guessing your double homicide didn't solve the problem?'

'No, it didn't rectify the situation. Other maniacs took their place, and the war happened anyway. So we went back even further to make our surgical incisions into history.'

'You murdered these people when they were kids?'

'No. Diana wouldn't allow us to do that. So we killed their parents before they became parents. But, of course, it made no difference. This was when Diana suggested we must observe all human history to decide which key points to manipulate. We noticed we weren't getting older, and my tumour had slowed its deadly incision into my brain by then.

'"We have all of time to get this right," Diana said. That's when we created the Watchers. And we observed, and we waited. Diana kept on with her experiments. Some girls rebelled and disappeared, and Ishtar and I became restless. And we noticed we were still ageing, but at a slower rate.'

'So you formed the Queens of Heaven as a faction inside the Watchers?'

'It was Ishtar's idea, not mine, but I was happy to go along.'

'At what point did you lose patience?'

Gloriana blinked and contemplated the question. 'When I discovered Diana was conducting secret experiments unknown to Ishtar or me.'

'That's when she brought a younger version of herself into her present – Daisy.'

'Their mother, my daughter Sari, had a problematic marriage. I only noticed this after Sari threw herself off those cliffs and into the sea.' She stared into the water as another punch floored my heart. 'It was from the exact spot our mother had done the same, but you won't remember that. Diana wiped it from your mind as she did with Daisy. Of course, it did nothing to alter Diana's terrible memories of the event, but when I discovered what she'd done, I convinced her to reach back and collect five younger versions of myself, including you.'

'So Diana and Ishtar are my granddaughters?' I said.

'Of course.'

She moved from the end of the pier and strode towards me. Gloriana held out her hand to help me up.

I refused the offer. 'And why did you do want five younger versions of yourself?'

'I was curious about her experiments, her theories it

169

might be possible to alter our present existence with subtle changes in our past.'

'Or maybe you wanted a group of girls you could control because they were you.'

Gloriana waved her hands in the air. 'You know we tried the cerebellum slicing on boys, but it did nothing but lobotomise them.'

She spoke as if talking about insects she'd squashed, her face a blank page.

'You're a monster.'

She grinned at me. 'That makes two of us.'

My guts ached, but the pain was seeping out of me. 'How did you get me and the others?'

'I didn't do it; Diana did. She started with me at Eighteen and then worked her way back to you, Fourteen. Seeing a younger version of myself was strange, but standing in front of five of you was bizarre. Thankfully, none of you freaked out, and once we explained how important you were to saving humanity, you were all keen to help.'

'By explaining, you mean you lied to us?'

Gloriana ignored those words. 'Do you remember what happened to Fifteen?'

'No.' I didn't hesitate with the answer.

She pursed her lips and shook her head. 'I think you do, Ruby. I think you blocked this one out because of your guilt.'

'Why should I feel guilty about any of your obscene actions?'

'Because what happened to Fifteen should have happened to you. You volunteered for the experiment, but she got in before you.'

The pain of the time jumps lessened in me, but a new

agony sprang through my flesh. I remembered about Fifteen. Now, when I didn't want them, the memories were returning.

'You'd lost faith in the Watchers, and you knew Ishtar and the rest of the Queens were plotting against you.' Impossible recollections rushed into my head. They were her memories, but I had them. 'You told the five of us this.'

Joy spread across her face like a disease. 'I couldn't trust the others anymore, so who else could I turn to but younger versions of me?'

'You wanted to create an army of you.'

'Exactly.' She rubbed her hands together with manic glee. 'Diana and I had succeeded in pulling younger versions of ourselves from the past, so we had to keep going and develop the experiment further. One of you would time jump ten seconds into the future and then fifteen seconds back again.'

'Leaving the future me with the older me before the older me became the future me?'

'Yes, a self-perpetuating time loop. That pattern would be repeated, adding ten seconds every time. All I had to do then would be pluck those versions of me out of their new realities and into this one. Of course, it was all theoretical and complex, but I read Diana's secret notes on the experiment and was determined to try it.'

'You mean you were determined for one of the teenage versions of you to try it?' I wasn't angry at her, and it worried me.

'I explained it to the five of you, and you were the first to volunteer. I didn't force it upon you.'

'So what happened to Fifteen?'

That detail was missing from my mind, and I knew it was for a good reason. But I had to know the truth.

Sadness engulfed Gloriana's eyes. 'The time between fourteen and fifteen was the worst in my life. You should thank us for erasing it from you.'

I didn't feel like thanking her for anything. 'Get on with it.'

'I won't go into details, but it made me wilful and rebellious. That rebellion forced Fifteen to perform all those time jumps the night before you were supposed to.'

'What happened to her?'

'Diana found her shaking on the floor. Fifteen was phasing in and out of her timeline. Having those different ten-second versions of herself together must have disrupted the time energy. The pain would have been excruciating. Then she split apart and disappeared in front of us. That caused Diana to hide three of my fragments and forced her to set you free from the control of the Watchers. You were always her favourite since you were my most naïve version. After that, she didn't trust me, and you were always the brightest version of me.'

'You don't know where Fifteen is?'

'It doesn't matter. Maybe she joined all those other missing girls, but she's probably dead now.' She gazed straight into my eyes. 'I'd craved death at fifteen, anyway.'

I wanted to leap up and punch her in the face. My legs pushed against the pier, but my body failed me. My stomach returned to normal, and I rose slowly, keeping my gaze on her at all times.

'You think changing the evolutionary process for females will benefit history?' I said.

I wouldn't admit to her that the idea was tempting even to me, not when the possible negative results could devastate all humanity. She strode forward and reached into her pocket. The laser gun was in her hand before I could move.

'I think you'll be back to your full strength in a few minutes.' She waved the weapon at me. 'You're pretending to struggle, but I can see your mind working overtime planning what to do here. You are a version of me, remember?'

'Nettie wants me to kill you.'

Gloriana frowned. 'That will be Ishtar's doing. She's given up on my world, on humanity's future. All she craves now is to control the whole of time. And after that, she'll try to understand how to step sideways into the fragmented realities and rule them. Then she'll take her army to conquer the rest of the universe.' She waved her arms in the air. 'The nuclear future awaiting this planet is of no concern to her now, not when she has many realities to play with. So even if you got rid of me, you'd still have her deal with.'

'All I want is a quiet life.'

'You don't wish for all your memories back?' She returned to brandishing the gun in my face. 'Because I can tell you about them.'

'You'd do that before you killed me?'

She turned away like a petulant child, moody and sullen. 'I admit I wanted to kill you once you ruined my plans in Tunguska, but you saved my life when I rolled over those cliffs.' Then, she was back to smiling at me. 'I woke to gaze at the sea rushing towards me before you brought us here. That must have caused you considerable pain, not only for your body.'

Her rant gave me more time to regain my strength. But I still didn't know what to do with her. 'Do you know when the tumour will kill you?'

Gloriana dropped her arms and put the gun away. 'The doctors on Kaladan offered to tell me, but I refused. It can't be long; I feel it pressing down on my brain. It could be a matter of weeks.' She gazed at me. 'Yet, it gives me time to do something significant.'

'Such as?'

'As if I'd tell you: you'd only try to stop me.' Her laugh was the low drone of a hummingbird. 'I think you'll have more challenging problems than me to deal with when I leave you here.'

She moved towards the end of the pier, never taking her gaze from me. The pain had vanished, and I was ready to stop her again.

'Whatever you do will have more negative consequences than good.'

Gloriana radiated confidence. 'No, that's not true.' Her eyes shrunk as she contemplated something. 'Maybe I'll spend the final moments of my life helping as many oppressed women and girls as possible.' Her teeth flashed white with a smile big enough to eat an exploding star. 'We will meet again before I die. And I think you'll beg for my help when we do.'

I lunged at her, but she vanished.

'Damn, damn and damn.'

I tested my aching bones and crept from where she'd stood. The sun was setting, and a yellow and orange haze reflected off the water. I staggered off the pier and stumbled onto the beach. My knees creaked as I bent my legs, dipping my fingers into the sea and pushing them down to the knuckles. The sea rippled around me.

I'd prevented Gloriana's plans, but it didn't feel like a win. Instead, an ocean breeze stroked my face as I stared across the waves and remembered the woman who'd been my teacher and friend.

'I'm sorry, Diana.'

I'd judged her without knowing why she'd done the

things she did. It was the same with my parents. They hadn't given me away, but my childhood must have been difficult if Gloriana had told the truth. If Nettie had kept her promise, I'd stopped Gloriana's mad design, and no matter what her parting words were, she wouldn't have the time or the resources to try anything like it again. Ishtar, the Queens, and the Watchers I would deal with later. It was about getting back to Dash, Daisy, and the others.

My recent painful journeys meant I shouldn't return to Siberia too close to when I'd left. My body couldn't take such agony so soon, but when escaping that place, there had only been fifteen minutes before the explosion.

Yet I had little choice and would have to deal with it. So I pictured the location in my mind and set the time for ten minutes after leaving on the morning of June 30, 1908.

Lightning flowed through the air as I landed. A massive wind burst from the side and knocked me to the ground. The surrounding roar was like a flock of banshees dying above me. I jumped up and scanned the area. It was empty of life, a column of bluish light as bright as the sun moved across the sky.

'Daisy!' I yelled, but I could barely hear my voice above the growl of nature.

The sky split in two above me, and fire screamed from it. I looked again for her or the others, scrambling forward against a fierce wind. My legs stumbled as I reached the river, tumbling down and hitting the mud. The heat rose from the water, steaming in front of my eyes and hurting my face.

I had to go. My mind was braced for the hop when a hand landed on my shoulder. Only it wasn't a hand but a paw.

'I waited for you.'

I jumped up and threw my arms around Dash as the thunder grew.

I cried above the noise. 'Where are the others?'

Blazing embers filled the sky. It wouldn't be long now.

Dash pressed her face into mine. 'I don't know. They were all gone when I awoke.'

You cannot trust her.

Gloriana's words about Nettie shrieked inside my head.

I shouted into Dash's ear. 'Return to base five minutes after leaving for the Blitz Club.'

We vanished as the world exploded above, arriving together under Stonehenge.

'Thank God you're back.'

Lucy threw herself at us, nearly knocking me to the floor.

How could I tell Lucy her daughter was missing? How could I tell her Daisy might not be her daughter?

'Lucy... there's something you have to know about Daisy.'

The wrench in my gut was worse than the pain I'd gone through after the rapid time jumps. She pulled away from us, a curious look in her eyes.

'I know.'

Daisy was behind her, stuffing cake into her face on the floor. I ran to her, scooped the kid up, and hugged her. When we separated, and I put her down, chocolate covered my top.

'How did you get here, Daisy?'

She wiped bits of the cake from her lips. 'I was sleeping, dreaming about you and Dash, and I heard your voice calling me, telling me to come home. So I thought about this place, and the next thing I was here. You weren't here, but Mum said you'd be back soon.'

Relief swept through me as I tumbled onto the sofa. Dash brought me a double gin and tonic, and I snatched it from her, swigging on it as she spoke.

'How could Daisy travel through time and space without your help?'

I grinned at her. 'Sit next to me, Dash. I've got a lot to tell you.'

Chapter 21

The End of Time

Daisy and Dash were safe. I'd thwarted Gloriana's plan, and no matter her threats to me, I doubted she could ever go back far enough to alter humanity's evolution. The Watchers weren't looking for me, and even though Ishtar and the Queens of Heaven were still out there, I could deal with them later.

There were other things I needed to clean up first.

I travelled one hundred years into the future to Avon, discovering as much as possible about Elric Oban. Then I went twenty years back to speak to the father, Victor.

'The inheritance you leave for your son gives him the means to inflict pain, torture and death on thousands.'

Of course, he didn't believe me. What parent would think their child could grow up to be a monster? So I took Victor Oban beyond his death and showed him what his son would become: we stood in the shadows as Elric plotted to conquer worlds, observed from a distance as he organised the torture of political and business opponents, and landed in the middle of the quake that would devastate large parts of the capital city. We didn't linger there long enough for Victor to hear the screams and witness the death and destruction.

Then I returned him to his time, leaving the decision to him as to what influence he would have on the future of Avon and the universe. If everything I'd learned recently about fragments of time were true, then the quake would still happen in one timeline, but I hoped I'd shown him enough to make sure it didn't happen in this one.

Different timelines.

Fragments.

I still didn't know how it all worked or if I could believe everything Gloriana had told me.

Gloriana – a future version of me. Or was I a past version of her?

And not the only one.

Nettie had taken the different versions of me somewhere. Should I try to find them? Would they grow up to be like Gloriana?

Would I become like her?

I gazed across the glistening city as I considered my own future.

Would I become a monster?

Thank You!

Thank you, dear reader for purchasing this book.

Many thanks to my wonderful wife for all her support and patience.

Extra special thanks to Karina Gallagher for being a dedicated reader of my work.

Cover design by James, GoOnWrite.com

About the Author

Andrew French lives amongst faded seaside glamour on the North East coast of England. He likes gin and cats but not together, new music and old movies, curry and ice cream. Slow bike rides and long walks to the pub are his usual exercise, as well as flicking through the pages of good books and the memoirs of bad people.

Find out more at www.andrewsfrench.com

Facebook:

https://www.facebook.com/A-S-French-Author-150145625006018

Twitter:

www.twitter.com/andrewfrench100

Instagram:

www.instagram.com/andrewfrench100

And replies to all his email at mail@andrewsfrench.com

If you have the time, please leave a review at Amazon or Goodreads

Thank you!

Ingram Content Group UK Ltd.
Milton Keynes UK
UKHW042034010523
421047UK00004B/38